D1001116

Sire Unknown

Sire Unknown

by Marjorie Reynolds
illustrated by Lorence F. Bjorklund

The Macmillan Company, New York
Collier-Macmillan Limited, London

The Macmillan Company, New York
Collier-Macmillan Canada, Ltd., Toronto, Ontario

Library of Congress catalog card number: 68-20608

Printed in the United States of America

First Printing

for
Audrey who gave me an idea and
for
Helen who gave me a word

Chapter I

"BEFORE THE SHOOTING STARTS, YOU'D BETTER PUT UP those No Trespassing signs, Jim," said Mr. Evans. "We don't want to have a lot of hunters wandering around and banging away at anything they see."

"You told me *you* were going to do it," protested Jim.

"Yes, I know," said his father, "but now I find I won't have time. I've made some appointments at farms in the next county, and tomorrow I've got to help Bill Morris get in our beans. *The Farmer's Almanac* says there's some bad weather coming."

"Just as soon as I get home from school you want me to start working. It's not fair," objected Jim,

"Well, why shouldn't you?" asked his father impatiently. "There's plenty to do around here." Suddenly his face relaxed and he smiled. "Ride your pony and carry a few at a time," he suggested.

"Oh, gosh, I want to take a regular ride. I don't want to carry a hammer and a lot of posters."

"Come on, get going," said Mr. Evans. "When people live in the country, there are certain jobs that have to be done. I've put everything you need on a bench in the barn."

"Okay," sighed Jim disgustedly.

"Thanks," said his father. "We don't want our pheasants roasting in someone else's oven, do we? Besides, they seem kind of like pets. Remember how we kept them alive by throwing out corn last winter when the snow was so deep they couldn't find food?"

Jim nodded. He didn't want their birds shot, and he hated to think of November, when men with guns would be out after deer. Recently, in the north pasture, he had seen a buck crowned with spreading antlers and a gentle-eyed doe, both standing stock still, heads up and alertly staring. It was not until he and his pony had come quite close to them that they had whirled, showing the white flags of their upturned, short tails. Fascinated, he had watched as with graceful bounds they soared over a wire fence into the adjacent wood. And the thought had crossed his mind, how could anyone shoot a deer, so free and beautiful.

Well, if the game on their farm was to be protected, apparently it was up to him. With a sigh of resignation, he started toward the pasture where his pony was turned out.

However, before he had gone more than a few yards, he stopped and called back to his father. "Shall I take the dogs with me?"

"Sure," shouted Mr. Evans.

Jim walked over to the kennel, a small shed with a wire enclosure attached, which was located just in back of the white clapboard farm house. Both the kennel and the house needed a coat of paint. If the bean crop turned out to be a good one, Mr. Evans had told Jim he planned to have the house painted. "Your mother would like to see the place spruced up a little," he had said.

"Come on, boys and girls, want to go for a ride?" called the boy, as he unlatched the gate to the pen.

A yelping, tail-waving avalanche of brown-and-white beagle hounds tumbled out of the kennel and jumped up on him.

"Hi, Tigger, hi, Tugger, hi, Lucy, hi, Penny," he greeted them, as he patted each head in turn and was assaulted again and again by yelps and leaps of joy.

"Come on!" he cried. And followed erratically by the little hounds who darted here and there seeking rabbit scent, he made his way to the pasture.

Standing near the gate was a light bay pony with sturdy legs and large, kind eyes who looked at him and nickered softly.

"Hi, Boots," said Jim. Before unlatching the gate, he stooped down and picked up a ripe apple that had fallen from a tree growing outside the pasture.

"Come on," he said. "I'll give it to you later," and he put the apple in his pocket.

Trailed by Boots, who followed him like a dog, and by the beagles, who, although making innumerable side trips, always kept heading in the right general direction, he soon arrived at the barn. Here, the whole procession trooped in after Jim, and he rewarded the pony with the apple, which he had broken in half. Then, instead of tying Boots up for saddling, he left him to wander about the barn with the dogs, who were running eagerly around whining at every new scent.

The barn was old. Cobwebs hung from the hand-hewn beams. The sills of the dusty windows were covered with chaff that had blown about when wagons had brought in hay. Along one side stood four box stalls, their heavy doors fitted with iron bolts; but of the four only one had straw in it, and was used by the pony at night.

Sometimes, in the darkness, when Jim went in the barn after supper to check Boots' water bucket and make sure it was full, he half imagined he saw among the moving shadows cast by his swinging lantern the ghosts of farm horses who used to be stabled here. Their names were lettered on the stall doors. DOLLY, BEAUTY, PRINCE, and BONNY. No one used horses on farms much any more. His father would borrow Bill Morris' combine to harvest the beans.

Thinking about his father and machinery made Jim remember the old beat-up car he drove. He looked so happy driving it that the sight filled Jim with exasperation. Why, he even called the old thing Finny, as if it were a pet or a friend. Once, the boy had shown his father a picture of a shiny red convertible he had found in a magazine. "Why can't we have a new car like that?" he had asked.

And Mr. Evans had laughed and said, "When our ship comes in."

By that, Jim knew he meant, "When the farmers buy enough Growquick fertilizer." Mr. Evans had the agency for three counties, and he was always on the road with his rattling car going from farm to farm. Last week he had told Jim proudly, "I have the best product on the market. They're buying more and more."

Instead of answering his father's enthusiastic remark, Jim had looked disgustedly at the old car and said, "Your fender's rusty. You'll come home without it some day."

Mr. Evans had looked at him tolerantly and remarked, "I'm not planning to drive up to the Ritz and impress people. All I want is to get around. The motor's fine, it runs like a clock. This car's good enough for a farmer."

But his father wasn't a real farmer. "I don't know enough about farming to make a success of it," he once had said. "Besides, fifty acres isn't enough land to make a living off of nowadays."

Jim realized that this was true. With the help of his neighbor, Bill Morris, who owned the combine, Mr. Evans planted a few fields of beans and together they cut two hay lots, but a good part of the land was wild and a haven for game.

His father loved the farm. He was fond of saying, "When old Cousin Charlie left me this place it was all the excuse your mother and I needed to get out of New

York City. We always wanted to live in the country.

Jim couldn't remember the city. He'd been only two when they'd moved here. The old, white clapboard house was home. Ever since he'd been able to walk, he'd played in this barn. He liked the barn smell, a mixture of grain, dusty hay, horse manure, and trodden earth floor.

Walking into the tack room, he pushed between old harness held together by rusted buckles and sniffed the musty smell of horse collars that sweat and age had mildewed. Roughly, he pulled his bridle from a peg. What a mess this tack room is! he thought. Dad doesn't care about anything in here. All he wants out of the barn is a place to park his car in the winter. Maybe he'd let me fix this room up. If he would, I'd paint it, throw out all this junk, and put pictures of horses on the walls.

As he lifted his saddle from the rack, the sight of the useless harness cluttering the pegs made him think once more of the animals who, in the old days, had patiently pulled farm wagons and plows. The whole barn seemed haunted, but nicely haunted, by a happy past when granaries had been full of harvested oats and corn, when sweating animals and hard-working men had made this a lively place. Now there was silence. He listened a moment but all he heard was the eager whine of the beagles, then a rustle and the sound of the pony chewing.

Boots stood where he had left him, munching on a bite of hay he had snatched from a bale. The beagles were dashing back and forth hunting the line of a mouse, while an offended-looking black-and-white barn cat sat high on the edge of one of the stalls and peered down at the hounds.

"Good old Boots," said Jim, setting the saddle on the pony's back. Ever since he was four, he had ridden this patient pony. Although it made him feel disloyal, he couldn't help thinking, You're nearly old enough to die. When you die, I'll bet Dad will buy me a bigger pony or maybe a horse. That is, if he can afford it.

He knew his father liked the idea of his riding. "I just hung around on street corners or played in the paved playground when I was your age," he had told Jim. "A boy should be in the country where he can feel grass under his feet and climb trees and wade in water. All the time when I was young, I dreamed of owning a pony. Now I can watch you riding and it's almost as if it had come true for me at last."

Jim had taken to riding like a duck takes to swimming. "You're a good old boy," said Jim, and he patted Boots' neck. Then he tightened the girth and slipped on the bridle. Checking to make sure that it fitted comfortably, he saw that the bit was just touching the pony's lips but not wrinkling them. Next, he tested the throat latch and nose band to see that they were loose enough for comfort.

On a bench beside the door Jim found the posters, hammer, and nails his father had left. He picked them up and led the pony out into a glorious afternoon of sunlight and autumn color.

Mounting was a problem with a hammer in one pocket and nails in the other and a bundle of posters tied together with string in his right hand. But Boots stood stolidly while he clambered aboard, and the beagles tried to hurry him up by yapping in various keys that blended together and made a kind of music.

As he rode along the boundary line of a cornfield where the dried and withered stalks had turned pale gold, Jim thought, Pheasants love to hide in the corn. Hunters know it and this is where they'll look for them. I'd better put a sign here. Dismounting from his pony, he tacked a No Trespassing notice to a big tree on the boundary line. Boots behaved like a bicycle; when you stopped him he stayed put, and the noise of hammering didn't frighten him.

Jim put the hammer in his pocket, hoisted himself astride once more, and gathered up his reins.

What a day it was! The maple trees were covered with red and yellow leaves so bright they seemed to shout with color. He passed a field of orange pumpkins almost ready for harvesting. As he rode by, he decided which ones would make good Halloween jack-o'lanterns. From time to time, he stopped and nailed one of his signs to a board on a fence post. Riding up a gradual incline, he came upon a vineyard where purple grapes hung on vines that had been touched by the first frost. These belonged to a neighbor but Jim was sure the neighbor would love him to have a couple of bunches, or at least that he *should* love him to have them. Leaning from his pony, he pulled at one of the

NO

vines until he broke loose a large cluster. Methodically, he began to detach the grapes one by one from their stems and to suck out the winey-tasting pulp, swallowing seeds and all.

Thoroughly content, the sun warming his back, he listened to the beagles making an excited chorus on the line of a rabbit between the rows of the vineyard. He was reaching for another bunch of grapes when he paused abruptly, feeling Boots stiffen. The pony's head came up, his ears pricked alertly.

Riding toward them, mounted on a gray pony, was the last person in the world Jim wanted to see.

Chapter 2

KICKING HIS GRAY PONY INTO A TROT, TUBBY CROFTON descended like the day of judgment on Jim.

Being fat and angry, he was out of breath. "You're stealing my father's grapes," he panted accusingly.

"I'm not stealing grapes. I'm just picking a couple of bunches to eat," said Jim, glaring at him.

"You should ask if you can take them," retorted Tubby.

"Oh, rats!" said Jim. "If your father's such a tightwad that he minds my helping myself to a couple of bunches of grapes, I feel sorry for you."

"He's not a tightwad. He's a lawyer and your father is just a fertilizer salesman. Fertilizer is like manure. Your father sells manure."

The words stung Jim like a lash across the face but he said quietly, controlling his temper, "Nothing grows right without fertilizer. How would you eat, do you think, without farmers growing things? My dad's job is very important."

"Why does he drive such an awful old car then?" asked Tubby.

These words struck too close to the mark for Jim to accept them calmly. With narrowed eyes he looked at Tubby's chubby face and said, "I'll bet your mother thought she'd borned a little baby pig when she first saw you."

Tubby's round face flushed, and he sat staring for a moment at Jim's erect and athletic figure sitting astride Boots before he selected his next verbal barbed arrow. Suddenly, his small eyes sparkled between their folds of fat flesh. "My father's going to buy me a real horse, one I can jump in shows," he announced. "I guess your father's too poor to buy you one."

"He is not!" shouted Jim. "Anyhow, I don't want a big horse. Boots is good enough for me."

"Good enough for you is right," echoed Tubby. "I'll bet you couldn't even *ride* a horse."

"I'll bet you fall off yours the day you get it," jeered Jim.

"Well, I won't," declared Tubby. "When you're fourteen years old, I'll bet you'll still be riding that shaggy old mop of a pony, and your father will still be driving that beat-up car."

The words sank like heavy stones into Jim's mind, and he couldn't think what to say to put Tubby in his place. While seeking for the right devastating remark, he was distracted by the sound of the beagle pack approaching in full cry. Looking down between the rows of grapevines, he saw the hounds coming, noses down, sterns up, led by a wildly bounding rabbit. The beagles were covering the ground so fast that their flying paws seemed a blur of speed, and their cries redoubled as they neared the kill.

Now they were right upon the two riders. The rabbit, blind with fright, gave a sideways leap and rushed heedlessly under the legs of Tubby's pony, followed by all the beagles giving tongue at the top of their lungs.

The gray pony, ordinarily a sedate and quiet animal, snorted with fright at finding himself a bridge over a fleeing rabbit and a whole pack of running hounds. Up

in the air he went and dumped Tubby like a sack of old clothes over the wire supporting the grapes.

From among the rustling leaves came muffled cries of "Help!" as Tubby struggled with the vines to free himself, while Jim laughed so hard he bent double.

"I'll get you for this," cried Tubby when he finally extricated himself and staggered to his feet. He shook his fist.

Jim stopped laughing. "I didn't do it," he said. "I can't help where a rabbit decides to go. Look," he said reflectively. "He got away. You made my beagles lose the line."

Tigger, Tugger, Penny, and Lucy were casting about frantically, panting and whimpering. Far off, somewhere in the underbrush, the rabbit had escaped.

"You're not hurt. Your pony didn't even run away," said Jim.

Tubby gathered up the reins and mounted. "I'm going to tell my father you were stealing our grapes," he said.

"Go ahead, stupid," said Jim, and with that they parted; Jim continuing on up the hill and Tubby cantering off purposefully in the direction of home.

For Jim, the day had changed. All the glorious color of leaves and orange pumpkins and yellow harvested corn now only spoke to him of summer's end. Soon there would be bare trees and whistling winds; a desolate cold November was near at hand.

I wish my father were a lawyer or a banker, he thought moodily. Why does Dad think he has such a great job, and why are he and Mom so happy jouncing around in that old car? If Tubby's going to be riding a real horse, he'll be looking down at me as if I were riding a dog. You're awfully old, Boots, why don't you . . . But he couldn't finish that thought. He laid a repentant hand on the pony's neck.

I'm not going to let that fat slob of a Tubby talking about a new horse get me down, he decided. He's always looking for a fight. Someday I'm going to give him a good punch in the nose.

He knew exactly when it was that Tubby had started to dislike him. In their year in kindergarten the teacher had put on a play in December. It had been entitled *Christmas Eve in the Kitchen*. Jim had been given the part of a rolling pin and Tubby was a fat lump of dough that he was supposed to roll out into Christmas cookies. Now that he thought about it, it seemed to him the teacher had been pretty dumb to make him roll back and forth over Tubby. All the children had laughed. Now Tubby never let an occasion go by without trying to make Jim uncomfortable. Why couldn't he just forget it? After all, the thing had happened years ago. It seemed silly to decide in kindergarten you hated someone and then keep it up for years. All Jim wanted was for Tubby to leave him alone. But that appeared to be an impossible wish, for on every occasion they met, Tubby tried to pick a fight. Jim decided it had become a habit by now.

Tubby thinks he's so great because he's got money and lives in a house with about twenty-five rooms and all that sort of stuff. I wish we lived in a big house like the Fitzgeralds, then I'd tell him where to get off, said Jim to himself. And he thought with envy about the Fitzgeralds' acres that adjoined the Evans' farm. Their huge stone house stood like a castle on a high hill.

For several years it had stood empty, looked after by a caretaker. In the past Mr. Fitzgerald's business had kept him in New York except for the months of July and August. During the last three summers, because Mr. Fitzgerald enjoyed good fishing, they had rented a house in Ireland instead of coming here. Jim remembered vaguely having seen the Fitzgeralds when he was younger. He was curious to see them again.

Some people have all the luck, he thought. Imagine being rich enough to forget about a house for all that time and then open it up when you feel like it!

Filled with discontent and resentment, he grudgingly finished his job of posting the land. But he had no desire to go home. Although he knew his mother would be worried, knew she had made a pumpkin pie for supper because it was his favorite dessert, still, he was in the sort of mood where he didn't care.

Maybe I don't really belong to them, he thought. Maybe I'm adopted. Maybe I'm really a prince. He tried to recall the details of a fairy story his mother had once read him in which the king's son had been stolen when he was a tiny baby and brought up by a swineherd, among the pigs. Then one day his identity was discovered. He was restored to the castle, and the king, his father, dressed him in purple velvet and hung a gold chain studded with rubies around his neck. "That would be the life," he said to himself.

He was roused suddenly from his self-absorption by a raucous sound and heard the air fanned by heavy wings. He lifted his head and saw three cock pheasants fly up out of a patch of chokeberry bushes. The harsh and startled sound they made reminded him of someone turning a rusty ratchet with a crank. Jim raised an imaginary gun to his shoulder. "Bang," he shouted, but was glad to see the birds settle down unharmed and run into a thicket of wild blackberry vines.

All at once he decided he was going to get rid of the heavy hammer weighing down his pocket. Then he would ride on and take a look at the lake which lay over a hill about a mile away. Pulling the hammer from his pocket, he dropped it on the ground. At the same time he marked the spot, so as to remember it, by noticing a large stone near the last posted sign he had put up.

"Come on, Boots," he cried. "Come on, hounds. Let's go exploring," and he squeezed the pony's sides with his legs, sending him off at a canter.

Feeling the breeze on his face and the rhythmic strides of the pony under him and watching the little hounds tearing along the ground trying to keep up put Jim into a better mood. As they started up the hill slope, he began once more to feel what a beautiful day it was and to take pleasure in the sights around him. Slowing to a trot, he passed by a clump of sumac and noticed that the leaves hung red and ragged like the feathers on an Indian war bonnet. Ripe milkweed pods had burst open and when he brushed against them, tiny brown seeds attached to silver floss went floating and drifting by in the air.

They were climbing steeply now and Boots began to breathe hard, so Jim slowed him to a walk as he started to climb the last of the rise. The pony's hoofs were digging into the ground and his legs were straining. The beagles' tongues hung out and he could hear their panting breath. All at once, they reached the summit and below them lay the lake contained within the rolling contours of hills. Sitting astride his pony, Jim imagined he was on top of the world and he felt like a god as he surveyed the wrinkled water below him, silver in the sunlight. Placid sheep grazed in a meadow nearby, and a flight of birds swooped past like a scattering of airborne leaves.

He had never before come upon the lake from just this angle and, as he looked about him, he saw he was standing within a few hundred yards of the huge stone house belonging to the Fitzgeralds. Part of the extensive lawns and gardens lay just to his right. Marigolds and late chrysanthemums bloomed profusely near a brick wall, and an old gardener was on his knees planting tulip bulbs at the edge of the bed.

From a door opening onto the lawn, two figures emerged and walked with the stiff and hesitant steps of the old toward where the gardener was working. The man carried a stick on which he leaned, and the old lady's arm was linked through his. There they are—

there's Mr. and Mrs. Fitzgerald, thought Jim. After a moment, the old man raised his head, noticed Jim, and pointed with his stick, apparently asking who he was. Jim whistled to the beagles, turned his pony, and started away from the edge of the garden feeling suddenly ill at ease and as if he had been caught spying.

Slowly descending the hill, with his face turned toward home, he thought, I'd like to see the inside of that house, and his imagination ran wild about what it must be like. Maybe you can press buttons that ring bells to make servants come running with anything you want. I'll bet all the rooms have big fireplaces with moose heads over them. Probably there are lots of billiard tables and gold bathtubs with silver faucets. It amused him to let his mind wander this way until he arrived home and had put the pony in the stable and the beagles in their kennel.

Not until he scraped his feet on the mat and opened the door of his own house did he remember the hammer he had left by the rock.

"Hello, Jim dear," cried Mrs. Evans, giving him a kiss. "I was a little worried. You're much later than usual. Supper's all ready; we were waiting for you."

"Well, I had to rub Boots down and feed him and water him. Then I gave the beagles some dog biscuits and filled their water dish. But I forgot the hammer," he admitted.

"That's all right, son," said Mr. Evans. "I don't think it will rain tonight. Pick it up tomorrow. Sit down, your mother's made us a good supper."

"I hope it's good," said Mrs. Evans. "They had a new kind of cheese at the store and I got some to go with the pie."

The clock ticked loudly on the mantel of the big country kitchen. The table, spread with a red-and-white checked cloth, had a bowl of yellow marigolds in the center. The room was warm, and the good smell of cooking made Jim's mouth water.

"Did you find any fences broken when you were nailing up the notices?" asked Mr. Evans, as he helped himself from a platter heaped with fried chicken. "Some of the posts in that fence that border the Croftons' vineyard are pretty rotten."

"No," mumbled Jim, a vivid picture of Tubby and the memory of Tubby's insults haunting him. "No, everything looked all right." Then he added, "I saw some cock pheasants."

"If we ever get right down on our uppers," said Mr. Evans cheerfully, "we could always live off the game on this place. Plenty of wood for fires, plenty of vegetables in the garden."

Mrs. Evans laughed. "Two big orders of fertilizer today and you talking about living off the land. I like that! Well, I could always make pies and sell them."

So long as they're in the country, they don't care what else they've got, thought Jim. They're always kidding each other like this. But I don't think it's funny. I'd like a new car and a horse and a big stone house and five dollars every week to spend on anything I want. Fat chance though.

Chapter 3

The morning was dull and overcast. The open season for shooting deer had begun. Jim's father had told him to keep to the roads when he went out on his pony.

"You never let me ride in the woods in November," complained the boy. "Our land's posted. Why do you think I might get shot? You don't worry when it's the pheasant season."

"Never mind," said Mr. Evans. "Just do what I tell you."

"Saturday, no school, and I have to ride on the road," grumbled Jim. "I want to explore. I want to go way back around the lake."

"You heard what I said," Mr. Evans replied.

A drizzly rain was falling as Jim left the house. Earlier, he had turned his pony out in the pasture and given him a pile of hay, because there was no longer sufficient grass to eat. But now he realized he might have made a mistake. What if Boots had rolled on the damp ground? He'd be covered with mud. I'd better get my raincoat out of the tack room when I saddle up, thought Jim, otherwise I'll get soaked.

Dimly, through the misty rain, he could see the pony standing stolidly in the middle of the field. Behind him were the woods where Jim usually started off on his rides. Bare, sapless trees lifted stiff branches toward the leaden sky and the oaks, to which a few russet leaves still clung, looked as if they were clothed in wet rags.

His eyes strained forward, trying to see if Boots was muddy and whether he'd have to do a major cleaning job on him. What was that moving among the trees behind the pony? He caught a flash of bright red. Not leaves, he thought, they're all withered now. Suddenly, the sharp crack of a rifle shot broke the morning stillness and, to his horror, he saw Boots throw up his head and fall to the ground.

"Hey, what are you doing?" shouted Jim, his voice full of anguish.

A man, clad in a red jacket, came to the edge of the woods, gave one look at what he had shot, and turning, began to run back through the trees. Jim had only a glimpse of him but he noticed his cap, black and peaked like a pixie's, not the usual hunting cap at all. He thought the man had a black moustache, but at that distance it wasn't possible to be sure.

"You've shot my pony!" screamed Jim, running toward Boots as fast as he could go.

Not stopping to open the gate, he scaled the fence, and, dropping to the other side, started running again.

Boots lay still, horribly still. Jim dropped on his knees beside him. "Oh, Bootsie, Bootsie," he sobbed.

Blood was running out of the pony's neck and staining the wet ground. How could even the stupidest person have mistaken him for a deer?

"Father!" screamed Jim, and he jumped up and started running toward the house.

Mr. Evans heard his cries and came to the door.

"What is it?" he exclaimed. "What's happened?"

"A man shot Boots!" cried Jim. "Get him! Get him! He's run away through the woods. He was wearing a red coat and a black cap."

"Did he kill him?" asked his father.

"Yes," sobbed Jim.

"I'll call the police," said Mr. Evans grimly. "He's had too much of a start for me to catch him on foot. He's probably in his car back on the highway by now." Quickly, he moved to the telephone and dialed a number. "I heard the shot," he said, "but I thought it was a truck backfiring. Now you see why I didn't want you to ride in the woods. Boots was so much the color of a deer." Holding the receiver away from his head, he stood looking anxiously at Jim who crowded up close to listen. When the telephone was answered, the boy could hear the policeman's voice. "State Police, Sergeant Stover speaking."

"This is William Evans. My farm's on Route 34 by the crossroads. A hunter has just shot my son's pony." Mr. Evans' voice was unsteady with emotion.

"Did you get his name?" asked the trooper.

"No," said Mr. Evans. "He ran away."

"Did you get his hunting license number?" asked the policeman.

"No," said Mr. Evans. "I wasn't there. It was my son who saw him. He said the man was wearing a red coat and a black cap."

"We'll have a look on the highway," said the policeman. "But I doubt if we'll find him. Most hunters have red coats. It's hard to do much if you don't have his name or number."

"I know you'll try," said Mr. Evans. "It was inexcusable. The pony was right near the barn." He hung up the receiver.

"I hope they shoot that man. I hope they kill him!" stammered Jim, sobs breaking through every word.

"Don't go out there again," said Mr. Evans, looking at his son with deep pity. "I'll get Bill Morris to help me bury him. You stay with your mother." And he went out the door, closing it carefully behind him.

"Come on, Jim," said Mrs. Evans, who had been standing in the background, her eyes full of tears. "Have a glass of milk." Gently, she touched his shoulder and guided him to a chair by the kitchen table.

Jim sat down and buried his face in his hands. Only yesterday he had been wishing for a new horse. Now, silently he thought, Oh, Bootsie, I really didn't mean it.

"Boots was old. You've had a wonderful time together," said his mother quietly. "He had to go someday. Come on, drink a little milk and you'll feel better."

Jim raised his head. Gropingly, he reached for the milk and took a few swallows.

"Have a cookie, they're fresh," urged his mother, and she pushed a plate of sugar cookies toward him. They smelled good but Jim shook his head. He wasn't hungry.

"I was doing some ironing," his mother said almost apologetically. "I think I'd better go on with it. The clothes are all damp."

Jim heard the thump of the iron on the ironing board, he smelled the fresh smell of newly pressed cloth. The clock ticked away. Once in a while his mother said something, but mostly she just let him sit and sort out his feelings.

It was an hour before Mr. Evans returned. "We buried him in the pasture," he said. "It seemed like a good place. He always enjoyed it there."

"Thanks," mumbled Jim, and he sniffed back tears that started to flow again.

"I want to get you a new pony," said Mr. Evans. He took out his handkerchief and blew his nose. "I was going to use the money from the beans to paint the house and do over the bathroom . . ." He looked at his wife.

"Never mind about that," said Mrs. Evans quickly. "We have a roof over our heads. Some things are more important than others."

"You need a new car," said Jim.

"What! Would you want me to get rid of good old Finny?" asked his father with mock indignation. "Impossible."

"Spring's a better time to buy an animal than winter," said Mrs. Evans.

"Here's an idea," said Mr. Evans. "We expect to breed Penny and Lucy this winter and their puppies will be born in March. We never have any trouble selling their litters at a good price. Now, you help us start the puppies on solid food when the time comes and clean out the pens and then you'll be earning money toward a new pony yourself."

Jim was staring straight ahead. "I think I'll take a walk," he said suddenly. He rose from his seat at the kitchen table and pulled his jacket off the back of the chair.

"What would you like for supper, Jim?" asked his mother. "Your father's going up to the village."

"I don't care," said Jim.

"Get a nice thick steak," whispered Mrs. Evans to her husband.

Jim went out the door. Slowly, with dragging feet, he walked toward the pasture. Even at a distance, he could see the bare patch of newly turned earth.

Chapter 4

A LONG, COLD WINTER HAD PASSED SLOWLY FOR JIM and made him realize how much time he once had spent with Boots. The hours after school dragged with no stall to muck out, no tack to clean, no pony to curry and brush and feed and water. He kept away from the barn.

No word from the police had ever come to say that they had apprehended the man who shot Boots. By now, Jim was pretty sure they had forgotten all about the case.

"Even if the troopers had been able to find him and then prove he was guilty, it wouldn't bring Boots back to you," said Mr. Evans. He was sitting at his desk putting pamphlets that advertised Growquick fertilizer into envelopes.

"I'd like to see him go to prison. I hate him," said Jim.

Mr. Evans shook his head. "If it had been a person who'd been shot, I suppose the police would have checked every rifle in the region and compared the marks on the bullet with the rifling in the barrel of each gun till they found the one that had fired the shot. But for a pony, I'm afraid, they wouldn't go to all that trouble."

"They should have taken the trouble. They should have tried to find out all they could," said Jim. "A pony's not just nothing at all."

Mr. Evans nodded sympathetically. Then he held up one of the pamphlets before slipping it into its envelope. "You know, fertilizer's a wonderful thing," he said. "In the old days when horses were used on farms instead of machinery, manure was spread on the fields to insure a good crop. Of course, people who have a herd of cows can still do that. In the old days when the Pilgrims landed, the Indians taught them to put a fish in each hill of corn."

"What good did a fish do?" asked Jim scornfully. Having asked the question, he knew at once he had made a mistake. Sure as fate his father would now start on one of his lectures about growing good crops.

"A fish has a lot of phosphorus in it. It's good fertilizer," said Mr. Evans. "The soil needs certain elements if it's to bear good crops. It needs nitrogen, phosphorus, and potash. Corn takes a lot of richness from the soil, and you have to put it back before seeding the next crop. It's good to rotate crops and plant something different each year. A field planted with alfalfa helps put nitrogen back into the land, and it's good to plow under corn stubble to give soil the kind of texture that will hold moisture. But most farmers nowadays need a good balanced fertilizer. Did you ever stop to think what would happen if the farmers got tired of farming? We wouldn't eat. I'm helping farmers, and that makes me feel my job's important."

Jim yawned. He'd better think up some excuse to leave, or his father was sure to begin talking again. "I guess I'd better feed the puppies," he said, and walked into the kitchen.

Opening a door to the cellar, he descended the narrow stairs carrying a bottle of skimmed milk he'd taken from the refrigerator.

The light was dim but he could hear a frantic squeaking going on in various keys. We must get them out of here before they're much older, thought Jim. They need some sunlight about now to make them grow strong and healthy.

As the puppies caught sight of him, they redoubled their treble yelps and clawed frantically at the wire that surrounded them. "All right. All right. I'm going to feed you," Jim assured them.

In one of the pens Lucy, who had a moment before been lying down and feeding her puppies, hopped over the low wire enclosure. She looked relieved to see Jim and wagged her tail. It was as if she were saying, "Thank goodness you've come to give them their main course. My milk's not enough now to satisfy these greedy puppies."

Jim went to a table that was pushed against the wall and set down the milk bottle. He pulled a chipped, blue-rimmed soup plate toward him and shook into it some puppy food as fine as baby cereal. This he mixed with a good quantity of milk and stirred it round with his finger.

Lucy had gone to the top of the cellar stairs and was whining and scratching at the door. "You're telling me it's Mother's afternoon out, aren't you?" said Jim. He ran up the stairs and opened the door. His father would let her outdoors, where she would play with Tigger and Tugger, who had been left alone in the kennel while Penny and Lucy were occupied in raising families.

The squeaking of the puppies now had redoubled into a frenzy of sound, and small paws clawed eagerly at the wire.

"All right, all right, I'm coming," said Jim. He glanced through a door into the furnace room, checking on another wired-off enclosure where Penny, who had had her litter two weeks later than Lucy, was lying placidly on her side. Ranged along her was a line of six tiny puppies. Little whimpers and sucks of contentment came from the wriggling bodies, each one seeking to keep its own place and not be pushed off by a brother or a sister.

In another couple of weeks I'll get them started on solid food too, thought Jim. Isn't it funny! Father birds help feed their young with insects and worms, and foxes kill a rabbit and bring it home to the vixen and her cubs. But imagine Tugger and Tigger dragging a box of puppy biscuits downstairs to help feed

their families! He picked up the plate of soft, runny food and stepped over the side of the pen to Lucy's litter.

As he knelt down on the scraps of torn newspaper that covered the floor, he was besieged by a scramble of small bodies, each trying to get a nose in the dish. Two were so eager they fell into the soupy mixture, paws and all, and Jim had to fish them out. One, a timid little creature, the runt of the litter, had been pushed completely out of the way. Even when Jim picked him up and set his nose beside the dish, the puppy appeared too bewildered to eat. So the boy stuck his finger into the cereal and offered it all coated, like a lollipop. The puppy began to lick. "I'm going to call you Weaky, you're such a weak little thing," said Jim, and again he offered the puppy his finger coated with cereal.

The telephone rang. Jim heard it through the ceiling of the cellar; heard his father's footsteps cross the living room floor, heard him answer with his usual cheerful "Hello."

He straightened up, holding the empty cereal dish in his hand. The puppies, their small bellies swollen with food, were quiet now except for little grunts of satisfaction. "Good-by, pups," said Jim. "See you next mealtime."

Stepping out of the pen, he carried the dish upstairs and took it into the kitchen where he washed it. "Dirty dishes make sick dogs," his mother had told him.

His father was still talking on the telephone. "Perhaps we might run over tomorrow morning about nine," he said. There was a pause, then, "Yes, we might be quite interested. Good-by," and the receiver clicked in place as Jim came through the door into the living room.

"That was a horse dealer named Sheldon who heard we were looking for a pony for you. He's got some new ones in and he wondered if we'd care to look at them."

"Hey, can we?" asked Jim. "Where does he live?" Secretly he was thinking, I hope he shows us horses, not just ponies.

"About twenty-five miles from here. He gave me directions how to find his place. We might take a look and see what he has to offer. I'm a little worried, though, that the kind of thing he has may be too expensive."

"Lots of horse dealers try to gyp you, I guess," said Jim.

"I'm afraid you're right. A good many of them seem to have earned that reputation, from what I've heard. I'll try to find out something about this man Sheldon," said Mr. Evans.

Chapter 5

IT WAS WITH A GOOD DEAL OF CONFIDENCE THAT JIM and his father drove up to the Sheldon stable on Sunday morning. A few telephone calls the night before had convinced Mr. Evans that this dealer was more honest than most and that his business had been built on a reputation for telling the truth about the animal he was selling.

"Wear your riding clothes," Mr. Evans had said to Jim. "You'll want to try the pony out if you find one you like."

The boy had put on his best tie. It was patterned with horseshoes and he had knotted it carefully. His hair was evenly parted and brushed smooth. Mr. Evans looked at his serious face.

"Well, here we are," he said. "Jump out and we'll see what Mr. Sheldon has to offer."

The owner was expecting them. He stood by the stable door slapping one booted leg with a lead rope.

His leathery face, worn by wind and sun, broke into a good-natured smile.

"I'm William Evans and this is my son, Jim," said Mr. Evans, extending his hand, which the dealer grasped cordially. Then Mr. Sheldon turned to Jim and gave him a bonecrusher of a handshake. "Come inside," he said. "I'll show you what I have."

With a sense of anticipation, Jim followed his father and the dealer through the barn door and saw a long aisle of concrete flooring with box stalls on either side.

"You said you wanted a pony," said Mr. Sheldon, eyeing Jim speculatively. Opening one of the doors, he snapped the lead rope onto the halter of the animal inside and led it out.

Jim's face fell. Before them stood a small and shaggy creature whose coat looked like a rug that needed vacuuming. "She's out of a Shetland mare by a Welsh stallion," said Mr. Sheldon.

"She's too little," said Jim quickly. "Boots was bigger than that."

"Yes, she's small—less than thirteen hands," agreed Mr. Sheldon. "She's a nice pony though. The boy who owned her has outgrown her, that's the reason the mare's for sale."

"She's smaller than Boots. I think he was thirteen hands," said Jim, who had once tried to measure his pony by laying his hands one after the other up the pony's leg to his withers. But suspecting that his own palm didn't measure the four inches called a hand, he had added a good many extra inches to his calculations.

Mr. Sheldon replied, "A pony can be fourteen-two; that is to say, fourteen hands, two inches. You probably know that. Anything bigger is a horse." He had led the shaggy pony back into its stall and unsnapped the lead rope. Now he shut the door and moved down the aisle. "Let's look at this one," he said. "He's about fourteen hands, I'd say."

A reddish-brown head peered over the stall door.

"Oh, he's a strawberry roan," said Jim, glad to be knowledgeable.

The pony, on being led out, proved to be a coarse-looking animal with a dish face. The dealer lifted the pony's feet one after the other to show how easy he was to handle around the stable. "He has a pretty hard mouth and his trot is rough, but he has a nice canter. You can see he does have a small splint on his off fore," said Mr. Sheldon, running his hand down the pony's leg, "but I don't think it will ever bother him."

Jim's eyes had strayed across the aisle to a delicate brown head with small ears and large, intelligent eyes. "What about that one?" he asked.

"Oh, that one," said Mr. Sheldon. "That's a horse. Fifteen hands. I see you're a good picker." He opened the door and led out the animal, whose coat had been well groomed and hoofs freshly painted with hoof oil.

"This horse is thoroughly trained and practically foolproof. I'd put any youngster up on him. He jumps well, too," he added.

"Is he a thoroughbred?" asked Jim. His eyes were shining as he ran a hand along the horse's neck.

"Dam a thoroughbred, sire an Arabian," said Mr. Sheldon. "His name is Barberry."

"How much are you asking for him?" inquired Mr. Evans quickly.

"Fifteen hundred dollars," replied Mr. Sheldon.

"One thousand five hundred dollars," repeated Jim, and all hope went out of his face.

"I'm afraid I couldn't sell him to you anyway," said the dealer. "I'm expecting a man and his son back this morning. They were here yesterday and asked me to reserve the horse until they made up their minds. I said I'd hold him for them until nine-thirty." He glanced at his watch. "They should be here any time now. I have a feeling they'll take him."

It was as if his words had been the cue for someone to enter. Glancing up at the sound of voices, Jim saw Mr. Crofton and Tubby walk through the stable door.

Strutting with the rolling gait of a barrel, Tubby walked up to the group. "How do you like my horse?" he asked Jim, giving a smirk.

"He's okay, I guess," answered the boy indifferently, but his face had turned palc.

Tubby pulled a candy bar lumpy with nuts from his pocket and unwrapped it. "Want a piece?" he asked, breaking off a tiny fragment and offering it to Jim.

"No, thanks," said the boy disdainfully.

Tubby took a greedy bite and began to chew. Sticky caramel oozed from the corners of his mouth.

Mr. Crofton, a small, thin man with a pinched, red nose that looked as if a clothespin had just been removed from it, turned on his son.

"Put that candy away!" he commanded in a harsh voice. "Aren't you fat enough without cramming your face full at ten o'clock in the morning?"

Hastily, Tubby rewrapped the remaining bit and was about to put it back in his pocket when his father snatched it out of his hand. "You're disgusting," he said, and threw the wrapped candy into a trash bin that was standing nearby.

Jim looked at Tubby, whose face had crumpled like a fallen soufflé. Gosh, he thought, averting his eyes, I'm glad my father doesn't speak to me like that.

Mr. Crofton pulled a checkbook from his pocket, and Mr. Evans moved along. A slight nod had passed between them a moment before. Mr. Crofton apparently couldn't quite remember who Mr. Evans was.

"Look, Jim, here's another horse. All the rest seem to be small ponies," said Mr. Evans who, having peered over the tops of several stall doors, had now stopped before a stall a little farther along. But when they both examined the animal inside, they saw he was a bony chestnut with a lackluster eye.

Mr. Sheldon had completed his business with the Croftons, put Barberry back in his stall, and accompanied Tubby and his father to the stable door, giving them his assurances that the horse would be sent round that afternoon. Now he came back to Jim and Mr. Evans, who were standing looking at the bony chestnut whose lower lip hung loose from his teeth.

"There's a nice quiet horse," he said. "Never shies, never bucks, never kicks. When you get a saddle on him though, he has more life than you'd expect. To look at him standing there, you wouldn't believe he can wake up, but he does. Cheap, too—only three hundred dollars."

Jim swallowed hard. Mr. Sheldon glanced at his

face. "You liked the one out of the thoroughbred mare by the Arabian sire, didn't you?" he said.

"Yes. Barberry," replied Jim.

"Well, he's sold, as you know," said Mr. Sheldon.

"Anyway, we can't spend that much money," said Mr. Evans. "Three hundred is about our limit." In his voice there was a note of apology.

"Humm," said Mr. Sheldon thoughtfully, looking first at Jim, then at his father. "How well does this boy ride?" he asked.

"He rides very well indeed," said Mr. Evans.

"Ever done any jumping?" asked the dealer.

Mr. Evans opened his mouth to answer "No" for Jim, but the boy interrupted.

"Not in shows or anything like that, but I used to jump Boots over logs and little fences," he said. "Nothing very high."

"Come with me," said Mr. Sheldon. "I have something that might do. You can look at him, anyway."

Chapter 6

WHAT SHETLAND PONY OR BONY, OLD, SWAY-BACKED wreck of a horse are we going to look at now? thought Jim bitterly, as he followed Mr. Sheldon out of the barn. He was tortured by a vision of Tubby riding Barberry and smiling disdainfully at him, mounted on some plug that was all his father could afford to buy. He walked along, head down, scarcely heeding where he was going and noticing only that they were moving toward a paddock surrounded by a white board fence.

It was muddy underfoot and a raw wind cut through his thin riding coat.

"Well, here he is," said Mr. Sheldon, and he leaned on the paddock rails and pointed.

Standing before them was a horse, partly white, partly brown, and mostly mud.

"I'm afraid he's been rolling," said Mr. Sheldon.

"He's a piebald," said Jim.

"No," corrected Mr. Sheldon, "he's a skewbald. A piebald is black and white."

"Is his sire a thoroughbred?" asked Jim hopefully.

Mr. Sheldon smiled. "No," he said. "I wouldn't be surprised if there's Indian pony back somewhere, and quarter horse, and maybe a thoroughbred grandsire." He pulled a paper from his pocket. "Let's see what it says about him," and he read aloud. "Skewbald gelding, fourteen hands-three inches, about four years old. Sire unknown, dam unknown. He came in a shipment from the Omaha stock yards."

"How much is he?" asked Mr. Evans.

"I could let you have him for three hundred and fifty dollars," said Mr. Sheldon. "Fact is, I haven't been able to sell him. He has two strikes against him. One, people around here don't seem to go for horses with patches. They like a solid color. It's partly, I guess, that when a horse like this one lies down in the stall, his white legs get all yellowed if the straw is dirty, and then you have to wash him with soap. People go for an appaloosa, they don't mind spots, but this white color with patches of brown, well, it's just not popular. Then there's another thing about him, after he takes a jump, he bucks."

"That would be dangerous," said Mr. Evans.

"Nothing mean about him, mind you. He only does it to play," said Mr. Sheldon, "but the average youngster couldn't stick with it. He's pretty small for a man to ride, and I couldn't honestly sell him to a lady or a kid as a thoroughly reliable jumper. If I had the time, I'd work with him. I believe he has a lot of potential. But I have a new shipment of horses coming in any day now and I want to make room for them. You'd be getting a real bargain, that is, if your boy's good enough to ride him."

A sound of feet squishing through mud made Jim, Mr. Evans and the dealer turn around. Tubby was puffing his way toward them. Where did he come from all of a sudden, wondered Jim. I thought he'd gone home.

"Mr. Sheldon," said Tubby, "Dad wants to know if we could buy one of your halters. We don't have one big enough for Barberry."

"Sure," answered the dealer. "Just keep the one he'll have on when he gets to your place."

Tubby was looking at the mud-covered horse. "What's that, a cow?" he asked, and he began to giggle.

Mr. Sheldon frowned. "This is a very good horse," he said. "All he needs is to be cleaned up."

"Well, so long," said Tubby. "Dad said he'd like the names of my horse's sire and dam if you'd please write them down."

Mr. Sheldon nodded, then waited until Tubby had walked around the corner of the stable. "Well, what do you say?" he asked. "Want to try him? Frankly, you won't be able to get much else at your price. This is a real buy."

"But he's dangerous," objected Mr. Evans. "I don't want to get my son something that will hurt him. He hasn't had the experience to ride such a horse."

So they think I can't do it, said Jim to himself. I'll show them. Aloud, he said, "I'd like to try."

"Good boy," said Mr. Sheldon. "As I say, the horse isn't mean."

"But . . ." objected Mr. Evans.

"I'll give him a hard cap to wear," put in Mr. Sheldor

"The mud's soft if I fall off," said Jim with bravado. He had been looking all the while at the horse, and the horse seemed to be looking back at him. Jim noticed he had a nice eye, brown and happy, no white showing to indicate an uncertain temper.

"Let's take him in the stable and brush him off a little," suggested Mr. Sheldon. "We'll saddle up in there." He opened the gate to the paddock and Jim followed him inside.

Instead of turning away, the horse took a few steps toward them and the dealer put a hand on his neck. "He's a real pet," Mr. Sheldon said. "I'd love to know who raised him. He's a very confident horse who's been well handled."

Jim stroked the brown patch between the horse's eyes.

"Lead him into the stable. Get to know him," suggested Mr. Sheldon.

The boy put his hand on the halter and stepped forward. Relaxed and at ease, the horse walked along at his side.

Inside the stable, Mr. Sheldon snapped the crossties to the horse's halter. He handed Jim a brush. "If you took care of your own pony I expect you know how to use this," he commented. "You and your father wait here. I'll get the tack." The bony chestnut watched over the top of his stall door as the boy brushed away at the caked mud. Presently, Mr. Sheldon returned carrying a bridle and saddle, which he set on the horse's back. "If you were going to ride for any length of time, I'd put on a sheepskin or a felt pad," he said, as with strong pulls on the billets, he tightened the girth.

"I'm giving you a pelham bit," he remarked, as he slid on the bridle. "A little more authority in it than a snaffle but not rough." He fastened the curb chain under the horse's lip and pulled gently on the bit to be sure he hadn't tightened the chain too much.

"There we are," he said. "Do you have light hands?" he questioned Jim.

"I think I do," replied the boy. "Boots had a good mouth."

"Well, let's go outside so you can mount, and we'll see how you get on with him," said Mr. Sheldon.

Mr. Evans trailed behind them, a worried frown on his face, his hands thrust deep into the pockets of his overcoat.

Mr. Sheldon held the horse while Jim mounted, then helped him adjust his stirrups.

"Just walk him around quietly in a circle," he said. "I'm going to get you a cap."

Jim gathered up the reins. He took a light feel on the horse's mouth and squeezed gently with his legs to make him walk forward.

There was a grace and fluidity to the horse's motion as he obeyed Jim's leg and hand signals, and they made a wide circle three times at a walk. He moves like a king, thought Jim.

"Here, try this on and see how it fits," said Mr. Sheldon. The boy stopped and the dealer came quietly to his side, holding a cap. The horse blew through his nose, pricked his ears forward, and looked at the black shape. As Mr. Sheldon offered the strange object to Jim, the horse shied a step away.

"He's only four. He hasn't seen everything. Steady boy, that's all right," said Mr. Sheldon quietly. He put his hand on the bridle and passed the cap to Jim. The boy dropped his reins and tried the cap on his head.

"It's okay," he said.

"Good," approved Mr. Sheldon and as Jim gathered up the reins, he removed his hand from the bridle.

"We'll take him inside the ring," he said, leading the way and he opened a gate into a fenced area where a few low jumps were set up.

Interested and alert, stepping lightly, the horse passed through and into the ring where a track near the rail circled the jumps. The ground was muddy and covered with hoof marks. Mr. Sheldon closed the gate; then, with Mr. Evans, went to lean on the rail.

"Trot him around," he called.

Jim gathered his reins a little shorter, pressed with his legs, and the horse went into a smooth trot. At the far corner of the ring, a piece of paper, probably dropped from someone's cigarette pack or candy bar, blew toward the animal's feet and he cocked his ears, raised his head, and shied. The movement took Jim by surprise because the horse had been going along so smoothly. But he kept his seat, didn't jerk on the bit, spoke quietly, "Whoa, steady," and soon they were trotting on as easily as ever.

"How about a little canter?" called Mr. Sheldon.

Jim, who had read a Pony Club Manual of Horsemanship and had practiced a few things on Boots, sent the horse off on the left lead and passed Mr. Sheldon and his father who were leaning on the rail to his right.

"Well done," he heard Mr. Sheldon comment.

The horse cantered with so much power and spring that Jim felt a little frightened by the amount of energy under him.

"Now walk," called Mr. Sheldon. Jim obeyed by gently pulling the animal to a trot then a walk, speaking to him all the time. "Whoa, steady, whoa. That's enough. Just walk now."

Mr. Sheldon, not bothering to open the gate, climbed the white board fence and walked over to one of the jumps and lowered it to about two feet.

"Just take him quietly over this," he said.

Jim's heart turned over. He swallowed. "Yes, sir," he said.

"Trot, then put him into a slow canter headed directly at the jump," called Mr. Sheldon.

Here goes, thought Jim. He felt happy and delighted and at the same time scared. But he did exactly what the dealer had said.

When they came into the jump he dropped his hands on the horse's neck, giving him a free head to take off, and leaned forward and gripped with his knees. The horse sailed effortlessly over the low bar and as he landed, put down his head and kicked up his heels. Jim fell off, right over the horse's shoulder, but he kept a hand on the reins and struggled to his feet.

The animal looked quite pleased with himself, as if it were all a game.

I want to get on again without Mr. Sheldon helping me, thought Jim, who felt foolish and knew he was covered with mud.

But the dealer appeared suddenly at his side and held the horse's bridle. "All right?" he asked.

"Yeah, I'm all right," said Jim. His hands were trembling a little.

"You must have something besides this to show us," called Mr. Evans.

The dealer led the horse, with Jim aboard, over to the rail. "That chestnut you saw in the stables is nice and quiet," he said. "I guarantee that he will jump two and a half feet safely. Now I grant you he's not much to look at and of course he's aged, about fourteen, I'd say."

Jim had put his hand on the neck in front of him and was stroking it. Inwardly and silently, he was talking to the horse. "You aren't mean, you were just playing," he said.

The thought of Tubby on Barberry and himself on the bony chestnut gave him courage. "I want to try again," he said.

"The boy has guts," commented the dealer approvingly to Mr. Evans as Jim moved away from them.

Once more he put the horse at the low obstacle, but this time he was prepared for what the horse might do. As his front feet touched the ground on the far side of the jump, Jim settled back in the saddle and gave a slight pull on the reins, at the same time yelling, "Stop it!" at the top of his voice.

It worked. At least for this one time. The horse

didn't buck and his sensitive, brown ears were back, registering astonishment at the loud yell that had come from just behind his head.

The dealer was laughing. "Well done," he commented, as Jim rode toward them at the fence and stopped.

Mr. Evans' face showed a mixture of pride and worry as Mr. Sheldon turned to him and said, "I'll make a deal with you. Pay me half the price now and if at the end of three months you decide that you want to keep him, then pay me the balance. If you find he's too much for the boy, if Jim's not happy with him, you can return the horse at any time. That kid's got the makings of a fine rider and the schooling he gives him will do the horse good."

"Can we?" asked Jim, turning to his father.

"Do you really want him?" asked Mr. Evans slowly. "He's quite a handful."

"Yes," said Jim, although way down somewhere, like a cold lump in his stomach, there was a very small *no* feeling. He wondered secretly whether outside of a ring he would be able to stop this horse if it took a notion to gallop on. Then, too, he was made uneasy by his vivid memory of Tubby calling the horse a cow. Who wanted to ride a cow? On the other hand, he was sure Mr. Sheldon had meant it when he had explained to them that you couldn't get exactly what you wanted for the price his father could afford.

"Well, then I guess it's a deal, Mr. Sheldon," said Mr. Evans.

Jim looked at his father, noticed his worn overcoat, and thought guiltily, Mother's going to go without having the house painted or the new bathroom, and Father could certainly use a new coat, not to mention a car. They're spending a lot on me because they feel so awful about Boots. Dad's got to spend three hundred and fifty dollars, fifty dollars more than he counted on.

But he pushed these thoughts aside, for he wanted a horse. Even though it didn't have a pedigree, even though it wasn't a lovely, silky brown like Barberry, he wanted a horse. And a horse with big brown cow patches was better than another shaggy pony and better than that sway-backed chestnut with the loose lip and dull eyes.

Giving a last pat to the brown-and-white neck in front of him, he dismounted. "What's his name?" he asked.

"The Guernsey," said Mr. Sheldon. "But you don't have to call him that. Give him any name you like," he said, noticing Jim's crestfallen face.

Holstein cows are black and white, Guernsey cows are brown and white, thought Jim. No wonder Tubby had kidded him. Everyone would be noticing his horse was the color of a cow. Why, someone with a sense of humor had even given him the name of a cow! He stood back and looked at him. Now that he was no longer on the horse's back feeling his power, his smooth gaits, he experienced the sort of shame that he felt when he looked at his father's old car.

Mr. Sheldon had been watching the boy's face. "Don't let those brown patches throw you," he said. "He has beautiful conformation. Look at those clean legs, and this fine sloping shoulder." He ran his hand down from the withers to the chest. "If you can ride this horse, you'll be a lucky boy to have him. I'd hoped to get a lot more for him. I'm sure he has tremendous potential but he's green. He'll take a lot of riding. Just stop thinking about Barberry. All this fancy pedigree stuff doesn't matter unless you're buying a race horse. Don't let that Crofton kid get you down."

How does he know so much? wondered Jim. How does he know Tubby burns me up?

"Just give him another name," advised Mr. Sheldon. "I'll deliver him to your house this afternoon."

Jim was silent as they walked toward their old car parked by the stable. He was remembering Mr. Sheldon's speculations abut his horse's breeding. Indian pony, quarter horse, and maybe a thoroughbred grandsire. The patches probably came from the Indian pony, thought Jim. He'd seen pictures of redskins on the warpath riding skewbald ponies bareback with nothing but a rope for a bridle. The Wild West. That would be the life! It must have been great racing over the plains on a skewbald pony shooting buffalo. Pow! Pow! Pow! Suddenly, as if a light had flashed the name onto a screen, he knew what he was going to call his horse.

"Apache Warrior!" he said aloud.

Chapter 7

Puppies for Sale PROCLAIMED THE FRESHLY PAINTED sign outside the Evans' house.

Jim had been hacking Warrior through the woods that afternoon and, before putting him back in his stall, he rode to the front of the house to see if the little beagles were getting too much sun in their pen on the lawn.

In the days when he was riding Boots he had always behaved as if he were on a bicycle, but with Warrior he had to be alert for any sudden move the horse might make. After all, he's only four years old, things frighten him, Jim told himself.

It had become his habit in the three weeks he had been riding his horse to watch closely what lay ahead of them, such as wash blowing on a clothesline, a scrap of newspaper caught and waving in the bushes, or even a chipmunk or a squirrel hurrying along about its business in the woods. Now, as he guided Warrior around the corner of the house, he kept a sharp lookout for anything that might surprise him.

But there was nothing unusual. The puppies were playing in their pen and this Warrior had seen before.

It was an exceptionally warm late April day. An apple tree near the kitchen window was covered with swelling buds that already showed a faint tinge of pink. The damp earth smelled of the rotted leaves and manure that had been dug deep into flowerbeds near the house. Bulbs were thrusting their green points up toward the sun. The daffodil buds were ready to burst into yellow flowers, and tulips showed green knobs that would soon turn into blossoms. In the steamy warmth, it seemed to Jim he could almost see everything growing taller.

Certainly the puppies had grown. Warrior lowered his head and examined them curiously as Jim stopped him beside their pen. This was Lucy's litter and he had given each puppy a name. There was Weaky, who was his favorite. Then Little Lucy, called that because she promised to have the same short legs and wide, intelligent head as her mother. Tiny Tigger had brown spots in the very same places as his father and then there was Butch, the biggest and huskiest one, and Funny Face, who had a round spot on her forehead. Jim dismounted and ran up his stirrups. The puppies welcomed him with yelps of joy, clawing at the wire and clamoring to be picked up.

"Here, Weaky, want to see Warrior?" he asked, and

he leaned over and put his hand under the stomach of the smallest pup and lifted him away from his brothers and sisters. The horse delicately sniffed the little, warm body. "Isn't he nice?" asked Jim.

After laying the soft head against his cheek, Jim put Weaky back among the other puppies. As he did so, he noticed that they had walked about in their water dish so that it was all muddy. He'd have to clean it out after he put the horse away.

I won't get on again. I'll just lead him back to the barn, he thought. He had pulled the reins over Warrior's head and he held them with his right hand close to the bit, taking the end of the reins with his left hand preparatory to leading the horse in. But the sound of a car stopping in front of the house made him pause. In the back seat he saw an old couple whom he recognized at once as being the Fitzgeralds. The driver of the car, he thought, was the gardener who had been kneeling by the flowerbed planting tulips on the day he had ridden to the top of the hill to look at the lake.

Jim saw him get out and go around the Rolls Royce limousine to the rear door, which he opened, and then stand aside. Slowly, Mr. and Mrs. Fitzgerald descended from their old-fashioned car. Their driver, who Jim now saw was indeed the gardener, helped them.

Mr. Fitzgerald advanced, leaning on his cane. His wife, her flowered hat trembling with the slight nodding of her head, was supported by the arm of the

chauffeur. Together they made their way to where Jim, holding Warrior, stood beside the pen.

"What dear little puppies!" exclaimed Mrs. Fitzgerald softly. Then looking at Jim with a smile, she asked, "How much are they?"

"The females are thirty-five and the males are fifty," said Jim.

"We would rather prefer a malc," said Mrs. Fitzgerald, "wouldn't we, John?" She turned to her husband.

"You're to choose exactly what you like, my dear," said Mr. Fitzgerald. Then he looked away abstractedly, as if bored by the whole proceeding.

"See that sweet little one there?" asked Mrs. Fitzgerald, pointing to Weaky. "Is that a male or a female?"

"It's a male," said Jim.

"He's the runt," declared the chauffeur.

"Oh, Campbell!" protested Mrs. Fitzgerald.

Jim looked at the man. He had a twinkle in his eyes, though his tone had been so abrupt. His back was bent from leaning over a spade for probably half a century, and his hands looked worn and callused. But when Mrs. Fitzgerald said she would like to look more closely at the puppy, Campbell leaned over and picked up Weaky as tenderly as he would have handled a petunia he was transplanting.

"Isn't he dear!" exclaimed Mrs. Fitzgerald. "What's his name?"

"I call him Weaky," said Jim, "but you can call him what you like."

"Dear little fellow," said Mrs. Fitzgerald, stroking the puppy's head with one finger then taking him from Campbell's big hand into her two small ones.

"This will keep you as busy as a grandchild would," said her husband half jokingly. "May I give you the money?" he asked, turning to Jim.

"Sure. That'll be all right. I can take it," said the boy.

Mr. Fitzgerald pulled out a wallet and with slow, stiff fingers, extracted five ten-dollar bills.

"I suppose you have a pedigree for him?" He asked the question as if he were sure of the answer.

"Yes," said Jim, "about a mile long. We couldn't sell them for so much if they weren't purebred. The litter's registered with the American Kennel Club. I'll ask my father to mail the puppy's pedigree to you."

"Why don't you ride that horse of yours up to our place some day soon and *give* the pedigree to us instead of mailing it?" suggested Mr. Fitzgerald.

"We know you know the way," said Mrs. Fitzgerald smiling. "You're the boy we saw on a pony last autumn. I'm sure of it. You had a whole pack of beagles with you."

"But you have a different pony, or rather now you have a horse," said Mr. Fitzgerald. "I suppose your pony became too small for you and you sold him."

"Boots was . . ." began Jim, but Mr. Fitzgerald had turned to the chauffeur. "Get that box out of the car please, Campbell," he said. "We'll put the puppy in it. We don't want any accidents on the seat on the way home." As he spoke his face wore an expression of distaste.

"Be sure to come up soon with the pedigree," said Mrs. Fitzgerald. "We want to find out all the impressive ancestors our little dog has descended from."

"Maybe I could come up tomorrow. It's Saturday," said Jim.

"Good," replied Mr. Fitzgerald. "We want to be sure the sire and dam are registered."

"But the boy says they are. I'm sure we can trust his word," exclaimed Mrs. Fitzgerald.

"Here, Campbell, put the puppy in the box," directed Mr. Fitzgerald.

"Say good-by to Weaky, Warrior," said Jim. "Say good-by to your brothers and sisters, Weaky. Be a good boy." Jim patted the puppy, who looked lost and frightened in the bottom of the deep box.

"I hope they'll be good to him," he said to Warrior, as he led his horse off toward the barn.

Chapter 8

JIM WAS NOT COUNTING ON BEING ASKED INTO THE Fitzgeralds' house. And even if they did ask him in, he knew he would have to refuse. Warrior was not the kind of a horse you could just tie up to a tree and expect him to stand quietly waiting for you. So when Campbell met him as he rode up to the door, he was neither disappointed nor surprised.

The man held out his hand and took from Jim the folded paper with Weaky's pedigree typed on it. "Mrs. Fitzgerald said to tell you she was sorry not to see you. The puppy squeaked all night in their bathroom. She and Mr. Fitzgerald are taking a nap to catch up on their sleep."

"Oh," said Jim. "I guess he was lonesome." Poor Weaky, he thought. It must have been scary for him to stay all alone in a spooky bathroom when he was used to lying curled up in a heap with his brothers and sisters. "Where is he now?" he asked.

"Out in the stable playing in the straw and getting

used to being alone," said Campbell. "I gave him an old shoe to chew on."

"I didn't know there was a stable here," said Jim.

"Yes," said Campbell, "over next to the garage. Only two stalls. Their boy, Robert, when he was a little chap, used to have a pony and Mr. Fitzgerald had a horse. They rode together quite a lot. Now Mr. Fitzgerald's too old and Robert has lived in Paris, France, for about fifteen years."

"Oh," said Jim.

"You didn't bring your dogs along today," remarked Campbell.

"No, my mother told me not to. She was afraid they'd run through the flower beds and rip up the daffodils."

"Want to look at the sheep?" asked Campbell. "You've come a long way with nothing to do at the end of it."

"Sure," said Jim. He didn't feel especially interested in sheep but he liked hanging around here, and he was amusing himself by imagining once again what lay inside the great stone house. Maybe there were secret doors and dungeons. His imagination worked freely, for he had read about castles.

The sheep, heavy with wool and supported by their thin legs and small, black hoofs, raised their heads and stared impassively while they chewed very fast with sideways motions of their lower jaws. Then they lowered their heads and began hastily cropping at the grass to get a fresh mouthful. Small lambs looking like toys played near their mothers.

"I don't suppose your dogs would chase sheep," remarked Campbell. "But some dogs do. It's a terrible thing if dogs get into sheep and start biting them. A sheep has no defense at all. The dogs just pull them down and kill them. When I was a boy in Scotland, I saw the ground all covered with blood and wool. And we never found the dog that did it."

Jim looked at the quietly grazing flock and shivered. His dogs would not do such a thing, he was sure. He wanted to see Weaky but he was afraid the puppy would beg to go home with him. So all he said was, "Well, I'd better be going. Say hello to Weaky."

"They call him Master Toots. A funny name, if you ask me," said Campbell. "I like a dog to be a dog. She's making a regular baby out of him."

"I guess Mrs. Fitzgerald's going to treat him like a grandchild," observed Jim. "Don't they have any grandchildren to play with?"

"No," said Campbell. "More's the pity. Robert and his wife have got a poodle in Paris." His mouth looked as if he were sucking on a sour lemon as he explained disdainfully. "They can't be parted from that blooming dog more than two weeks. That's as long as Robert ever visits his family. But at least he does come once a year. Mrs. Fitzgerald's sentimental about dogs just like her son. You watch, she'll be turning that sporting little beagle into a house cat. She'll overfeed him and pet him to death. Give me a dog that's a dog," muttered Campbell, this time with more emphasis.

"Well, I'd better be going," remarked Jim for the second time, and he gathered up his reins.

"Ride over any time," urged Campbell. "The dogs won't hurt the flowers. Bring them along. It's quiet here. I like a bit of life." He pulled a short pipe from his pocket and began filling it with tobacco as Jim rode away.

What a wonderful place this would be to live, thought the boy as he took one last look at the handsome house standing like a castle among its ancient trees, green lawns, and bright flower beds. Imagine being able to go into that house and walk from room to room and sleep between silken sheets. Why, it would be just like the prince who had been brought up by the swineherd, Jim said to himself. Supposing I were like that prince. Supposing I really belonged in the castle.

A wild imagining flashed into his mind. He knew his mother and father had gone to France on their honeymoon. He'd always been told he'd been born in New York, but perhaps his parents weren't telling him the truth. Perhaps, and here his mind took another wild leap, perhaps Robert Fitzgerald and his wife had had a baby boy they didn't want. They met Mr. and Mrs. Evans in Paris. "We are dog lovers. We don't like children," they had said. "We'll give you one hundred dollars if you'll take this baby off our hands and back to the United States with you."

Suddenly Jim laughed out loud. Good grief, he thought, I'm making up a TV thriller! I wouldn't believe it if I saw it.

But the next second he remembered having heard someone say that real life was often stranger than made-up stories. Who could tell?

Jim came out of his trance of imagination with a jerk. He could feel Warrior gathering himself as if for a big shy. Something was frightening him. In his bemused state, Jim had ridden as far as the path that led into the woods. Now he heard the sound of a trotting horse, and Tubby came into view.

Warrior, who had stopped and was standing still as a frozen statue, head up, ears forward, began to relax when he saw what was making the trotting sound he had heard long before Jim.

"Hi," said Tubby, as they met. "Want to canter around a field? Or are you scared to canter your new horse?"

"Of course I'm not scared, what do you think?" replied Jim.

"Maybe we can find something to jump," suggested Tubby. "Or doesn't your cow jump?"

Jim clenched his fist and rode at him.

"Hey, take it easy!" exclaimed Tubby, backing Barberry away. "I was only kidding. What's your horse's name anyway?"

"Apache Warrior," said Jim.

"How's he bred?" asked Tubby. "I'll bet his dam's

not a thoroughbred. I'll bet his sire's not an Arabian stallion. He looks to me like some kind of a painted circus horse."

"He has wonderful breeding," said Jim, thinking fast. "His sire's name is Tomahawk, the famous Western stallion. Haven't you ever heard of him? Where have you been all your life? His grandsire was, let me think . . . Oh, yes, Arrowhead, the famous horse Chief Sitting Bull used to ride."

Tubby's eyes were wide with wonder. "Are you kidding?" he asked.

"Why should I be kidding?" asked Jim.

"Who was the dam?" asked Tubby, his eyes narrowing suspiciously.

"Who was the dam?" asked Jim. "Let's see. His dam was Rebel, a direct descendant of Traveler, the horse Robert E. Lee rode in the Civil War."

"Traveler was a gelding," said Tubby flatly.

"Oh, that was before he got to be a gelding," said Jim. "It was while he was still a stallion."

"I think you're telling a big story," said Tubby. "Look, here's a fence. Do you want to jump it?"

"Sure," said Jim, with more bravery than he felt, and eyeing the three-foot post-and-rail fence that separated the woods from a grassy field. The fact was, he had taken Warrior over only a few very low jumps since he had brought him home, and those were ones he'd set up in back of the barn. The horse had bucked him off twice. But more and more he was acquiring the knack of getting Warrior's head up at the right moment.

"Want me to give you a lead?" asked Tubby.

"No," said Jim. "Don't worry, I'll go first." As a matter of fact, he was afraid Warrior might get excited if he saw a horse jump in front of him. Then he probably would kick his heels high and throw his rider off for Tubby to laugh at.

Gritting his teeth and settling himself down in the saddle, Jim cantered toward the jump then leaned forward just before Warrior took off. As the horse landed, Jim could feel him try to get his head down, but he checked him by a quick tug on the reins, at the same time yelling, "Stop it!" in a frightening voice.

"What did you yell at your horse like that for?" asked Tubby, who had caught up with him and was cantering along by his side.

"I just said, 'Hop it,' so he'd jump it," said Jim.

"But he *had* jumped," said Tubby.

"Well, maybe I said it a little late," agreed Jim. The last thing he wanted was for Tubby to know that he was worried about Warrior bucking him off.

"Let's walk now," said Tubby, who was puffing so hard his cheeks went in and out like balloons.

Jim had some trouble slowing Warrior down. But Barberry came back to a trot, then a walk at Tubby's command to "Whoa."

Twenty yards farther on, Jim was able to stop, and there he waited until Tubby caught up to him.

"That's kind of a wild horse you've got there," said Tubby. "I thought he was running away with you."

"No, he just likes to gallop along," said Jim.

"Say," remarked Tubby, "there's going to be a horse show over at the fair grounds. I'm entered in the Junior Class."

"How high will the jumps be?" asked Jim.

"Nothing over three feet. They'll be cinchy," said Tubby. "Dad says he's gotten me a good horse and he wants me to win. I probably will."

"Maybe I'll go in for it too," said Jim in an offhand way. "What day is it going to be?"

"Saturday, May twenty-sixth," said Tubby. "Dad's had a carpenter put up some barrels and painted jumps so I can practice."

"I think I'll come over to your house and practice too," said Jim.

"Not much, you will," said Tubby. "Why should I let you practice over my jumps? I want to beat you."

Jim fell silent.

"Dad had the jumps made while we were away at Plymouth, Massachusetts," said Tubby. "He took me to see the *Mayflower*. That's the boat the Pilgrims came over on. My grandmother and grandfather were Pilgrims. My grandfather was the captain."

"What was his name?" asked Jim. "It couldn't have been your grandfather," he added. "The *Mayflower* landed in 1620."

"I forget his name," said Tubby, "but he was the captain and he was my great-great-great-something grandfather. We bought post cards. I'll show them to you some time," he offered graciously. "I'll show you a picture of the boat my great-great-great . . ."

"Oh, dry up," said Jim. "It's not the real boat. It's just a fake they sailed over from England about ten years ago."

"Well, I don't know . . ." began Tubby. But just then Warrior shied violently at a rabbit that jumped out of the woods.

Jim found himself half out of the saddle, his arms around the horse's neck.

"He's only four years old. He's learning," he gasped, as he hauled himself back to where he was supposed to be sitting.

"Well, come to the show so I can beat you," said Tubby. "I've got to head for home now."

"Good-by," growled Jim.

As Tubby left him he gave a hard look at Barberry. It was impossible to deny that here was a fine-looking horse, but Jim tried to fault him. Of course he had to grant that the horse's manners were perfect, but he considered after a careful look that Barberry's neck was too short and his back too long.

Jogging along toward home, he once more began to think about the wild conclusions to which his imagination had led him, and he began dreaming up a scene that became more and more real as he thought about it. One day, when Robert was visiting the Fitzgeralds, Jim would confront him with these words: "I am your long-lost son." And his father would grab his arm, look into his eyes, and cry, "Yes, Jim, it's you. I think it's you. Do you have a brown mole on your left side?" And Jim would pull up his shirt and show the mole and his father would say, "I realize now I always wanted a son. How could I have let them take you away?"

They were nearing the barn and passing the tree where he used to pick apples for Boots. A large black crow flapped out of the branches and startled Warrior, who swung like the hand of a clock from twelve to quarter past. Jim landed on his back in the grass.

Oh, well, he won't run off. He'll just go into the barn, he thought.

As he picked himself up, his lips were pressed together in a firm line and he vowed inwardly, I'm going to do a lot of practicing over jumps so we'll beat Tubby. We've just got to beat him. He makes me sick with all this business about his ancestors and his horse that's got a sire that's this and a dam that's that. I'll show him who has the best horse.

Chapter 9

The County Fair grounds were probably the worst place Jim could have chosen to start Warrior jumping in a show, he soon realized. From the moment they arrived there, the strange sights and smells kept the horse in a state of wary apprehension. Music blared, the ferris wheel turned, paper bags popped, voices shouted, children ran about with balloons and pinwheels, horses whinnied, and trucks backfired.

Tubby had stationed himself beside the horse show ring and was using Barberry as a grandstand. Sitting slackly, his reins loose, he watched the touch-and-out class.

Jim stood quietly nearby, holding Warrior and waiting until it was nearer the time to go in before he mounted. His tack had a fine polish from the good rubbing he had given it the night before, and the horse's coat shone from a thorough grooming. He had washed his white legs with soap and water until there wasn't a trace of yellow stain, and he had worked on the brown patches until they were as shiny as shoes.

Both horses had been trucked over by Mr. Sheldon, and the man had given Jim this bit of advice. "Don't force him too much and don't frighten him. Today will be a good experience, so there's nothing to worry about if he doesn't do well. I'm pleased with the way you're getting on with him. He's not an easy animal to ride, by any means, but he has a lot of potential. When once he really settles down, I feel confident you'll have an outstanding horse."

"Hey, there's going to be a lot of people in our class," said Tubby, turning to Jim and motioning with his hand.

Boys and girls, some with pale and pensive faces, some smiling and relaxed, were hanging about in the vicinity, some mounted, some dismounted. One little girl, her hair done in pigtails, her teeth visibly chattering, kept a tight pull on her pony's mouth. The patient animal, finally becoming tired of the strong tug on his bit, backed up and bumped into a restive bay horse who lashed out with both hind feet, just missing Warrior's flank. Jim hastily led his horse away, deciding to mount and ride off at a distance from the crowd. Mr. Sheldon had told him, "Either stand and hold a horse or ride about on him, but don't use him for an easy chair." Which is just what Tubby's doing this minute, thought Jim. He knew he must warm up Warrior and get him going smoothly before entering the ring. His number was fourteen on the program, but two horses had been scratched, so he figured he would be the twelfth one to compete. Tubby was wearing Number Fifteen and would be the last competitor in the class.

Gathering up his reins, Jim prepared to mount, but Warrior sidled about nervously, making it impossible for him to get his foot into the stirrup.

Suddenly, a steadying hand was laid on the horse's bridle, and he saw his father standing in front of him, smiling encouragingly.

Jim swung onto Warrior's back and looked down at Mr. Evans. "Thanks," he said. "This place upsets him. He was going quietly at home."

His father nodded. "I wish I knew more about riding so I could give you some pointers. I can do better with a truck than a horse, I'm afraid. In the army they used to call on me if a jeep acted up, but I've never understood horses very well." Jim sensed that his father was looking at him sympathetically, understanding his nervousness.

"Good luck," he said. "Don't worry if you don't win anything. I know you'll try your best and that's what counts."

Jim didn't answer. He gave a smile so faint it was only a quiver of one corner of his mouth.

After looking about, he found a comparatively open space of trampled grass and dusty ground and began trotting the horse to limber him up. Warrior carried his neck arched, his ears pricked forward, and every step he took seemed tensed by apprehension. But gradually, under the boy's quiet voice and light contact with his mouth, he began to relax.

Jim heard his class announced. "Junior riders, first entry is Number One, Daffodil, owned and ridden by Cathy Trench."

"It's a long time before we go in," he told Warrior, and he slowed the horse to a walk trying, over the crowd, to see some of the jumps he would so soon be taking. It worried him when he noticed they were all painted bright colors. There were blue-and-red barrels, a white picket fence with red stripes, and a board fence decorated with a purple and yellow bull's-eye. Not one simple rail fence among them. The jumps, shining with new paint and many of them decorated with pots of geraniums, were not the sort of thing Warrior had ever seen before.

Jim felt suddenly overpowered by a lonely feeling, for he feared he was almost certain to make a spectacle of himself before all these people. And there was nothing he could think of to buck himself up. His father had driven him over in an old wreck of a car with fertilizer bags piled high on the back seat; he himself was riding a horse that had been named after a kind of cow. But Warrior didn't even know some people thought his patches were kind of funny. He didn't mind that he had no pedigree. He thinks life's a ball, Jim told himself. I'm the only one who worries.

Suddenly, he became conscious of the assured and powerful stride of the horse under him. "Let's try to show them what we can do," he said. At that moment, he felt an overwhelming rapport with his horse and as if together they must succeed. Impulsively, he dropped his cheek onto Warrior's mane in a gesture of confidence.

Glancing up abruptly to see where they were heading, he noticed the Fitzgeralds' old-fashioned car approaching, driven by Campbell. On the back seat sat Mr. and Mrs. Fitzgerald with Weaky between them looking fat and cheerful. The puppy was wearing a collar studded with rhinestones.

Oh, my, aren't you leading the soft life! You look like a poodle, thought Jim, and he wondered whether Weaky, or rather Master Toots, was really enjoying himself. Perhaps not so much as his brothers and sisters who had been sold to families he was sure would give them a chance to run about and get into trouble and be real dogs.

A man selling souvenir flags of the fair paused beside Jim, who had stopped his horse to watch the Fitzgeralds go by. "Say," he remarked, "that's a swell-looking old couple. And look at that 1932 Rolls Royce. They ought to be stuffed and put in a museum."

"They're friends of mine," said Jim proudly. "They bought one of our dogs." But the man didn't stop to listen. He was moving on and calling out, "Flags, souvenirs, genuine, official souvenirs. Get your flags here. Half a dollar. Cheap at the price."

"Friends of mine," said Jim over to himself. "Maybe more than friends. Maybe even my grandmother and grandfather." He watched the car park beside the horse show ring and realized that in a few moments he would be appearing before them. It gave him a sort of confidence and identity to imagine himself related to these rich and important people.

Once more he trotted Warrior to make him responsive and supple. Quite a strong breeze had come up and was raising puffs of dust that made his eyes blink and water. He pulled his hat down on his forehead so as not to lose it. Turning, he moved toward the ring and waited to hear his number called.

Mr. Crofton was standing at the gate beside Tubby, his hand on Barberry's neck. "You go in there and *win*!" Jim heard him say.

The next horse was being called. "Number Fourteen, Warrior. Owned and ridden by Jim Evans." The gate swung wide and Jim found himself walking his horse slowly into the ring.

The first jump was a gray wall painted with black lines to simulate stones, and on the posts at either side teetered pots of red geraniums.

Jim put the horse into a slow canter on the right lead and circled him until they faced the jump. The moment Warrior saw what blocked his way, his head went up, his neck stiffened, but he kept moving forward under the strong pressure of the boy's legs. He's going to go, Jim thought jubilantly.

But just then a puff of wind unbalanced one of the pots of geraniums which sailed off its post and landed in front of them.

Warrior stopped dead and Jim almost went on over

his head. A murmur of sympathy came from the spectators as he pulled himself back into the saddle.

One of the judges walked forward, patted the horse's neck, and spoke to Jim. "Bad luck," he said. "Try again." And picking up the broken pot and the flowers, he carried them over to the rail and dropped them on the ground.

Jim started Warrior cantering again but the minute the horse found himself facing the jump, he stopped dead. Then he began to back up, with the mincing gait of a circus horse, and the crowd in the grandstands began to laugh. Jim pressed the horse's sides with all the strength of his legs. He pressed his weight into the saddle and, moving back and forth, tried to urge the horse forward. But nothing Jim could do would make Warrior budge a step in the right direction. A whistle blew and he knew he was disqualified.

Tubby passed him going in as he went out.

Mr. Evans met Jim outside the gate. "Too bad," he said. "You know, we haven't made the final payment on this horse. We could send him back."

"No," said Jim. "It wasn't his fault. He's young and things surprise him." His cheeks were burning from the sound of the crowd's laughter.

"I remember," said Mr. Evans, "when I was a boy my father telling me a true story about a doctor's horse.

"The horse's name was Victor and he was very brave and spirited. One wild and stormy night with the rain pouring down, the doctor was driving home after calling on a sick child and he came to a wooden bridge over the river. Usually Victor trotted right over that bridge, making the planks rattle. But this night he stopped dead. And he wouldn't move, even though the doctor lashed his back with a whip. So the doctor got out of his gig, carrying a lantern. In those days they didn't have flashlights, of course. And he went to Victor's head to see what was the matter with him. Well, do you know, to the doctor's horror he saw that the river, swollen by the rain, had washed the bridge away. The horse had saved his life." Then Mr. Evans grinned at Jim. "Maybe that's what Warrior thought he was doing for you. Somebody seemed to be hurling geraniums at you and he decided to keep you out of range!"

Jim smiled back at his father, with quick appreciation of his understanding, and just at that moment, Tubby came huffing and puffing out of the ring with Barberry perfectly under control. Mr. Crofton was standing there to meet him. "You knocked down the pickets on that gate," he said accusingly. "Why didn't you warm up before you went in, Mr. Know-it-all? You thought you had such a good horse it wasn't necessary. Right? Right? Am I right?" His voice rose in anger.

Jim turned Warrior away and Mr. Evans walked by his side abreast of the horse's shoulder. "Look here," he said, "Sheldon was telling me there's to be a small show in August. A sort of Hunter Trial with natural jumps. He suggests you go in for that."

"I will," said Jim. "I'll practice. I've got to beat Tubby. I'll bet he won that class even though he made one fault."

"No, he didn't," said Mr. Evans. "A horse called Daffodil went clean."

Jim felt a small sense of satisfaction. "Gee, Mr. Crofton's rough on Tubby," he said.

"Mr. Crofton has what I guess you'd call the will to win," commented Mr. Evans.

"But it's not him that's winning. It's Tubby," objected Jim.

"It's the same thing for some fathers, I think," said Mr. Evans.

"Why is Tubby so fat when his father's so skinny?" asked Jim. "His mother's kind of little and skinny, too."

"A throwback, I guess, to some portly ancestor," said

Mr. Evans. "Lots of times children don't look like their parents. It's all a question of genes."

"What are genes?" asked Jim.

"Ask your teacher," replied Mr. Evans. "All I know is, they combine before a baby's born and give it the characteristics it's going to have. Blue eyes, curly hair, crooked teeth, all that sort of thing."

Jim checked Warrior to allow a car to pass in front of them. It was the old Rolls Royce and Mrs. Fitzgerald was holding Weaky up to the window. "Stop, please, Campbell," she ordered. "I want to speak to Jim Evans.

"Here's our dear little man. Here's Master Toots," said Mrs. Fitzgerald.

"Does he still squeak at night?" asked Jim.

"Mercy, no. He's as quiet as a good little mouse." Then turning to Mr. Evans she said, "Your boy's a fine rider. It was hard luck about the plant falling off."

"Yes, hard luck," echoed Mr. Fitzgerald from the depths of the car.

"Come up and have a cup of tea with us on Friday afternoon, Jim," she urged. "We've taught Master Toots a trick and we'd like to show you. Campbell will put your horse in our stable. I assure you he'll be quite all right."

"Thanks," nodded Jim. He swallowed a bubble of emotion that had risen in his throat. "Thanks. I'll be there just as quick as I can make it after school."

Chapter 10

"I KIND OF WISH I WERE GOING TOO," SAID MRS. EVANS. "I'd love to see the Fitzgeralds' house. Remember and tell Dad and me all about it at supper tonight."

"Okay," said Jim. He glanced at his mother and felt critical of her appearance. Dressed in rust-colored slacks and an old shirt of his father's, she had just come into the kitchen after weeding the flower beds in front of the house. A smudge of mud dirtied one of her cheeks, the breeze had rumpled her hair, and her fingernails were black from the soil in which she had been working. She looked blissfully happy.

Motioning toward the window over the sink, she called Jim's attention to the apple tree outside. "Did you ever see anything like the flowers we had on that tree this year!" she exclaimed. "It's going to bear a lot of fruit. I'll have to get you and Dad to prop up some of the limbs or the weight of the apples will break them."

"I guess so," said Jim.

"We don't want to lose that tree," said his mother. "They are the best apples for pie. Better than the red ones on the tree by the pasture. And these golden apples are *so* beautiful to look at," she added dreamily.

"I've got to go," said Jim, and he started moving toward the door.

His mother's glance shifted from the window, and she began to inspect him critically. "Have you cleaned your fingernails," she asked, "and have you washed your face? You could have brushed your hair a little better."

"I'm okay," said Jim, jerking his head sideways as she made a move to smooth his hair.

"I think it's really very nice of the Fitzgeralds to ask you to have tea with them. Remember not to sit down until Mrs. Fitzgerald sits down. Be helpful and polite, and be sure and pass things if they want you to."

"Okay, okay," said Jim hastily, and he left his mother without a backward glance. Thank goodness he'd gotten away without her kissing him. She kissed him in front of people sometimes, which was the worst.

Never before had he saddled up so fast. Warrior was put into a canter by Jim almost from the moment he mounted, although he knew he should have walked and trotted him for a least a quarter of a mile.

It won't hurt him, he thought. Not just this one time. Half believing the story he had made up, he thought, The son of Tomahawk is tough, he can stand most anything. But he did let the horse walk up the steep hill to the crest of the Fitzgeralds' property.

Below him he saw, as always, the splendid view of the lake where small, gaff-rigged boats, their white sails puffed out by a strong breeze, scudded like one-winged birds across the blue water.

Having in the past had the stables pointed out to him, he rode in that direction. Campbell, on his knees, a short-stemmed pipe between his teeth, was weeding a rose bed beside the drive.

Hearing the sound of hoof beats, the man slowly straightened up. "You're riding that horse now as if you feel very happy on him," he remarked. "At the horse show you were sitting kind of tense."

"I don't really like shows much," said Jim, "but there's somebody I've got to beat. I practice jumping every day. We're jumping four feet now."

"Don't forget the old saying, *Throw your heart over the fence*," advised Campbell. "If your horse feels you're determined to jump after your heart, he'll usually go on."

"Warrior loves to jump," said Jim. "I think he could be a champion high jumper. It's just whether I can stay with him."

"You're a good rider, boy," said Campbell. "I liked the way you handled things when your horse got scared of those geraniums. Some youngsters would have flailed around with their legs, as if they were beating carpets. You just sat there and squeezed and used your body.

Never mind if he wouldn't go that time. You handled things the right way."

Jim felt pleased. This man understood horses. Without any anxiety, he handed Warrior over to him.

"They're expecting you. Just ring the front doorbell and you'll be let in," directed Campbell, as he led the horse away.

Jim walked across the lawn which smelled sweetly of clipped grass. The windows of the house stared at him coldly, and he felt rather shy. Mounting the broad stone steps to the door, he half wished he hadn't come. The doorbell was hard to find but when he did, and pressed it, there was silence. Perhaps somewhere off in the depths of the house, it had rung and notified whoever was going to let him in.

While he waited, he turned and looked out toward the sheep pasture, but the sheep were not there. He wondered whether they had been sold.

When the door was finally opened, he was standing with his back to it but at the sound, he faced around and saw a small woman, not Mrs. Fitzgerald, dressed in a plain, black dress and a white apron.

"Come in," she said. "Mr. and Mrs. Fitzgerald are expecting you."

Jim stepped forward and his first impression was of an overwhelming vastness. Immensely high ceilings, tall windows, huge Oriental rugs, all made him feel that both he and the maid were very small indeed as he followed her where she led. They passed a large fireplace in a room full of chairs and sofas. On a table he noticed a graceful bunch of fresh flowers. Books lined one of the walls, but on the others and over the fireplace hung portraits in massive frames. The room was full of the lingering incense of winter fires and the perfume of summer flowers.

The maid continued walking before him. She led him through a door and into a small, cozy sitting room where Mrs. Fitzgerald sat in a high-backed chair behind a low table on which tea cups and saucers had been placed. Never before had he seen her without a flowered hat, and her head looked small and silvery.

Mr. Fitzgerald rose from the corner of a comfortable-looking sofa, took his glasses off his nose, and put down the magazine he had been reading. "Good afternoon, Jim," he said.

Master Toots, full of importance, leaped from the depths of an easy chair and ran toward the visitor whom he instantly recognized and showed it by trying to claw his way up Jim's leg.

Mrs. Fitzgerald held out her hand, and the boy went to where she was seated and took it. "How do you do," he said blushing.

But Mrs. Fitzgerald quickly put him at ease. "That little dog will never let you alone unless you go and sit in his favorite chair with him. But when Clara brings the tea, why don't you move right over here by me so you will be near the cakes?"

Jim did as he was bidden and, with Master Toots on his lap, began to feel more at home.

"How was the ride over?" asked Mr. Fitzgerald. "I used to spend many pleasant hours on my horse years ago riding over the fields and through the woods."

"It was okay. Where are your sheep?" asked Jim. His eyes were traveling about the room and noticing handsome old colored prints of sailing ships that hung framed on the walls.

"The sheep are in another pasture over the brow of the hill. You can't see them except from an upstairs window. Do you like sheep?"

"Well, not so very much," confessed Jim, "but the lambs were cute. Campbell showed them to me."

"They're growing up now," said Mr. Fitzgerald. "By the way, I see you are looking at my ship prints. I have some ship models you might like to take a look at later."

"Were you ever a sea captain?" asked Jim.

Mr. Fitzgerald's mouth twitched with amusement, and Mrs. Fitzgerald answered for him by saying, "He was president of the Atlantic and Pacific Steamship Line, but he retired last year."

Jim nodded. That must have been an important job, he thought. No wonder they live in such a fine, big house.

Just then Clara, who proved to be the woman who had opened the door for him, came in with the tea. She arranged everything in front of Mrs. Fitzgerald who lit a small spirit lamp under the hot water kettle. "Lemon for you, John," said Mrs. Fitzgerald, pouring out a cup and passing it to her husband.

"And how do you take your tea, Jim?"

"Two lumps and cream, I guess," stammered the boy, who had never had tea before but remembered what his father took in his coffee.

"Come over here and sit by me," directed Mrs. Fitzgerald. "I see Clara has made some cream cheese-and-jelly sandwiches, and these chocolate cakes look nice and rich."

Jim, who was now feeling more at home, left Master Toots and went to sit by his hostess.

"We must show you our little dog's trick," exclaimed Mrs. Fitzgerald enthusiastically. "Master Toots, sugar time," she called.

The puppy leaped from his chair, ran to the tea table, sat down, and barked twice. "There's my good little man," said Mrs. Fitzgerald, praising him and handing him a sugar lump. "Isn't he bright?" she asked Jim. "So young and yet so quick to learn."

"Pretty good," agreed Jim politely. They're going to ruin his teeth for sure, he thought.

The tea was hot but when he could put it to his lips, the warmth gave him a pleasant feeling, and it tasted good. He found the sandwiches and cakes delicious. Maybe Campbell is giving Warrior a snack of something back at the stable, he thought. The memory of having cantered so soon after leaving the barn gave him a twinge of guilt, and he hoped the man had walked his horse up and down a bit before putting him in a stall.

"Come on and look at my ship models," said Mr. Fitzgerald, rising from his chair.

Jim set down his empty cup, brushed some crumbs from his lap, got up, and then looked anxiously at the rug where they had fallen. He glanced at Mrs. Fitzgerald. "Thank you," he said awkwardly. And he followed Mr. Fitzgerald out of the room and across the hall to enter another rather small but high-ceilinged room that appeared to be Mr. Fitzgerald's study. Enclosed in glass on bookcase shelves stood several full-rigged models of sailing ships. But the thing that caught Jim's eye was a painting that hung over the fireplace of a man on a horse and a boy about twelve years old mounted on a pony.

Jim stared at the picture. Mr. Fitzgerald had started to explain some feature of one of the ship models when he noticed Jim was not paying any attention and that his gaze was riveted on the portrait.

"My son and myself," he said.

"He lives in Paris," murmured Jim.

"Yes, he's lived there for a good many years," said Mr. Fitzgerald. "Now this ship model is an exact replica of the *Flying Cloud*," he explained, turning his back on the picture.

Jim wanted to ask more questions, but the subject of his son did not seem to be one Mr. Fitzgerald was anxious to pursue.

Before turning away, Jim took another long look at

the boy in the portrait. Brown hair just like his own. And the way the boy sat his pony was exactly the way Jim imagined he himself must have looked on Boots.

Mr. Fitzgerald appeared to sense Jim's lack of interest in the ship models and to notice how his eyes kept straying around the room as if he were seeking some-

thing else. Abruptly, he stopped talking and stood a moment.

"Well, Jim," he said, "I think we'll go back to the sitting room and say good-by to my wife. She and I are both going to take a short rest now before dining out. It's been good to see you." And he led the way back to where Mrs. Fitzgerald was tidying up the tea tray, making it ready for Clara to carry away. With her heavily ringed hand, she picked a small piece of chocolate cake from one of the plates and gave it to Master Toots. Then she looked up smiling.

"Good-by, Jim," she said, holding out her hand, which he shook gravely. "We've enjoyed your company, and I think you can be pleased with the way your puppy is behaving himself."

Mr. Fitzgerald led the way through the large drawing room.

"Do you have any secret passages?" asked Jim.

Mr. Fitzgerald must have been a little hard of hearing, for he replied, "No, we have no partridge, but we have quite a few pheasants on the place."

Jim didn't pursue the matter but followed the old man's slow steps out into the hall. Here Mr. Fitzgerald opened the front door for Jim and, at the same time, happened to glance down at the floor. "Look at that!" he exclaimed with exasperation, frowning and pointing to a damp stain on the rug near the door. "That dratted puppy's made a puddle. I'd like to take him by the neck and throw him into the rose bushes. That would teach him!"

Jim wanted to say, "He tried to get out. The door was shut." But he sensed that Mr. Fitzgerald was not the kind of man to whom you offered unsolicited opinions.

As the door closed behind him, he drew a deep breath of free air. The grandeur, the formality, the strangeness of the house had impressed upon him the feeling of having had an adventure. But he was glad he was going to eat supper in the cozy kitchen at home. He began to wonder whether the boy in the picture had liked living in that house. Why had he gone to Paris to live? When the old man's composure had been broken so suddenly and harshly at finding the puppy's mistake, Jim, for a moment, had been almost afraid of him.

Chapter 11

IT HAD BEEN A HOT, UNCOMFORTABLE NIGHT, AND JIM awoke sticky with perspiration and wondering what time it was. Darkness obscured the familiar shapes in his room. He could barely see the bureau over which hung a pennant of Niagara Falls, or the chair where he had carelessly flung his clothes, or the bookcase on which paraded his collection of china horses. The luminous clock on a table by his bed showed it to be eleven-thirty. But there was no sound of ticking. During the night the clock must have stopped. He had forgotten to wind it.

Moving restlessly, Jim tried to shake off the dream from which he had awakened. Tubby and he were at a horse show, and Tubby was dressed in handsome riding clothes and polished boots. Barberry looked bigger than life-size and ready to jump anything. On the other hand, Warrior seemed to have shrunk and felt weak under him. Where his ears should have been, there were cow's horns. Looking down at his riding britches,

Jim saw that they were covered with spots, and his boots had gray, dried mud on them. Tubby said, giving him a condescending look and a superior smile, "My horse is by an Arabian stallion out of a thoroughbred mare and we're going to beat you and your cow."

Before Jim's mind's eye the dream was enacted again as clearly as if it had really happened. But the strangest part was that he could remember exactly what he had been thinking when he woke up, because the words seemed out of a book and not what he would really think or say. Wonderingly, he repeated them over to himself. "He tries to cut me down to size, but I am, by my own estimation, of so small a size that when he is through, there is really very little left of me."

Impatiently, he rose up in bed and looked at the window. Wasn't the darkness lightening a little? As he sat staring, he heard a cock crow and then the sleepy cheep of a waking bird.

Flinging back his rumpled sheet, he leaped out of bed. I'm going to ride and jump, he thought. We're going to jump every fence in the countryside so Warrior will do well in the show on Saturday.

Dressing hastily, he crept from the house after leaving a brief note on the kitchen table. HAVE GONE RIDING.

The air outside felt fresh, and it seemed hard to believe that yesterday the thermometer had registered ninety-two degrees in the shade. Dawn was breaking and he heard again the triumphant notes of a cock hailing the rising sun which, as yet, did not show above the eastern horizon.

Going into the barn, he was conscious of the hush of night. Shadowy and still were the heavy rafters, the bales of hay, and the massive stall doors. And again, as so often before, he experienced a ghostly sense of the presence of the old farm horses. Is that why Warrior is content out here by himself, he wondered. Perhaps he doesn't feel really alone.

As he passed the stall marked Prince, where Boots used to live, he remembered his good pony. Careful not to pinch his fingers, he unbolted and swung back the door of Beauty's stall and there in the half darkness and deep straw he found the alive, comforting presence of his own horse.

"What a horrible dream I had!" he said. "You sure don't have horns, Apache Warrior. You are an Indian chief in war paint, and we're going to beat that sissy old Barberry." Affectionately, he ran his hand down the horse's neck, beginning to be proud of the patches, imagining a bold warrior, his face daubed with paint put on to frighten his enemies.

When he led his horse outside saddled and bridled, he saw the sun had risen. Wisps of foggy vapor shrouded the trees making them look like phantoms.

Jim glanced back at the farm house. The shabby paint looked whiter than usual in the morning light. The beagles had heard him and were yelping in the kennel, wanting to be let out to follow him on his ride.

But he decided not to take the little hounds, although he didn't like to disappoint them. I'm always watching them while I'm jumping to make sure they're not on the other side of the fence, he thought. Today we're really going to practice and they'd just be a nuisance.

Mounting, he rode off through long meadow grass feeling in the freshness of the dawn the promise of another hot day.

Yesterday when he had called Mr. Sheldon to ask whether he would truck his horse over, they had talked about the upcoming show. "It's really a Hunter Trial," the man had said. "The fences will be natural. A sportsman named Mr. Cakebread has laid out the course on his place, and people will simply sit in their cars or on the hillside to watch. It's not a bit like the horse show at the County Fair, with grandstands and all that sort of thing. But the jumps will be a good bit higher."

"How high?" Jim had asked him.

"There's nothing over three feet nine, but there's a triple bar."

"What's that?" Jim had inquired.

"Three bars set up one in front of the other and increasing in height, the last one being the highest. You take them all together. The whole thing measures about five feet across, I'd say, and the highest part is three foot six. It's necessary to go at it pretty fast to clear it."

Jim knew his father felt nervous about the idea of his jumping, so in order not to worry him he had set up a makeshift triple bar out in the woods. It was flimsily constructed, and not a very safe jump but it was the best Jim could make working by himself. Although he knew that a horse faced with a good solid obstacle will pay more attention because he knows he can't knock it down, still, Jim didn't worry, for his horse hadn't given him one refusal since the County Fair.

By now, Jim had the greatest confidence in Warrior. The regular exercise he was giving him, combined with his firm correction of him by word and rein, and once even with a whip, had made him stop the hard bucks he used to give after a jump. However, Jim always permitted him a little bounce of joy to celebrate the pleasure of flying through the air. The weeks they had spent together had made them understand one another well. Jim recognized Warrior's desire to play, and the horse understood by now about how far he could go without being punished. "You're a rascal," said Jim, patting his neck after they had jumped the fence into the woods and Warrior had shown his joy in jumping by giving his usual bounce.

Faced with the triple bar, he pricked his ears forward and gathered himself, ready and eager to go. A horse who did not enjoy jumping might well have plowed right through the lightly balanced poles and come down with legs tangled in a broken fence. But for

Warrior, any excuse to jump was enough to make him want to soar, and he and Jim sailed the triple bar in fine style.

"Just do it on Saturday," implored Jim, patting the brown patch on the horse's neck. "Don't get worried in a new place. At least there won't be any geraniums."

They continued on and came out into the north pasture after taking a low fence.

The day was becoming hotter by the minute and the air had a sultry quality. Jim looked up into the sky and saw dense, white thunderheads of clouds. It occurred to him that he might turn around and go home, but he rejected the idea. Still half in the grip of his nightmare, he felt the need to be brave. He wanted to try out his courage and his strength. If a big storm was coming, let it come.

As he rode along, he saw the leaves on the poplar trees shaking like a shower of silver coins. The wind was rising.

Lately, as if pulled by a magnet, he often was drawn in the direction of the Fitzgeralds' place. When he had described his afternoon there to his parents, he had told them he expected to be invited back soon, but he hadn't been. However, just being in the vicinity of the great house stimulated his daydreams, and for a brief time he could feel a sense of identity with these rich people who impressed him so strongly.

Today he approached the property from another direction and soon came to a wire fence enclosing a pasture. For some time as he rode along he had been hearing the sound of furious barking, and now suddenly he was shocked and dismayed to find out what was causing the excitement.

In the field before him he saw a large, black dog running the Fitzgeralds' sheep. The helpless creatures, frantic with terror, were dashing along, their small hoofs thudding on the hard, trodden ground. Behind them the shaggy, black dog, yapping with excitement, snapped at their heels. Jim shouted but the dog didn't appear even to hear him. He looked for a gate but the field was very large; the gate must lie over the brow of the hill, and he couldn't see it from where he was standing.

Suddenly, to his horror, he saw the dog grab one of the sheep, pull it down, then go for its throat.

"Oh, no!" cried Jim. "Stop it!" But he might just as well have been commanding the wind.

Now he knew he must get in there. But how? He couldn't ask Warrior to go over wire. A horse needs something it really can see in order to jump. Besides, the wire running along the top was barbed and the thought of how Warrior could rip the delicate skin of his legs if he jumped too low, or how he might tear his shoulder if he fell into it, made Jim shiver. He himself had once become entangled in a barbed wire fence and he remembered the nasty gash it had given his arm. His instinct was to run on foot but he knew he mustn't leave Warrior tied to the wire because he could get himself caught. Frantically, he looked around for a suitable tree where he could hitch his horse, but he couldn't see one. In the meantime, the dreadful, bloody work was going on in the pasture. At any moment the dog might dash after another sheep and pull it down and then go for still another one. Something had to be done, but what? Suddenly, he knew that somehow he must jump that wire and get to the sheep.

A desperate idea had occurred to him. Unbuttoning his shirt, he ripped it from his back and holding it in his hand, he rode close to the fence. "See, Warrior," he said. "It's a jump. It's this high," and he laid his shirt over the top of the wire.

Then he rode a few paces away, headed his horse straight at the spot where his shirt hung, and put him into a canter. Giving a great squeeze with his legs, he drove him at the barrier with all his will and determination.

The horse, who always welcomed any opportunity to jump, judged his moment of takeoff beautifully, and they sailed over the treacherous fence and landed in the sheep pasture.

"Good boy," breathed Jim between clenched teeth, and he didn't even correct him for the mighty bounce of joy, almost a buck, that he gave on landing.

Thundering across the field, they bore down on the black dog and the struggling, bleating sheep. Jim had no plan except to ride the dog down. He had no whip, nothing but Warrior's iron-shod hoofs.

A thought flashed through his mind. A horse won't

step on anything alive if it can help it. "I'll make him step on that dog," he muttered fiercely.

The black dog's muzzle was buried in the sheep's wool, and he was so intent on his kill he didn't even look up. Jim, driving his horse along and giving the kind of yells he imagined Apache Indians gave on the warpath, came straight at them. "Step on him, Warrior!" shouted the boy. But the horse, with a great leap, tried to jump the struggling pile of gray wool and black hair. He would have succeeded if the dog had not at the last second taken fright and leaped away in front of the galloping horse. There was no way for Warrior to avoid him. He landed with one of his hind

feet on the dog's leg, and a yelping and howling began such as Jim never before had heard.

Warrior had become excited by Jim's yells and the all-out gallop they had had after jumping the fence, but Jim finally stopped him and rode slowly back. It was hard to tell how badly the sheep was hurt. A sheep fallen on its back can't get up. But the dog obviously had a broken front leg and with yelps of pain was hobbling on three legs trying to get away.

What shall I do? thought Jim. He had begun to tremble violently in the letdown after his surge of courage. Licking his dry lips, he sat staring at the dog he had injured.

Just at that moment a loud shout caused him to look up, and he saw Campbell approaching as fast as his old legs would carry him. Waving a heavy stick in his hand, he was calling, "Well done, boy, you got him. Good for you."

Warrior shied away from the waving stick, and Campbell dropped it to the ground and approached more slowly.

"I saw it," he panted. "I saw it all but I couldn't come any faster." His gnarled hands were pulling the sheep over and onto its feet. "In another minute he'd have killed her," he said. "The heavy wool at her throat saved her life, but she's bitten bad."

"Oh, that dog!" he cried, shaking his fist at the howling, limping creature that had by now moved a few yards away. "I know who he belongs to. I've had my eye on him. I'll get the dog warden and that devil will never bother sheep again, that's for certain."

"What do you want me to do?" asked Jim.

"Ride up to the house and go to the kitchen side," directed Campbell. "Clara's in there. Tell her I said to call the vet and the dog warden and that they're to come to the big sheep pasture. Tell them Mr. Fitzgerald wants them to hurry. Fast."

"Mr. Fitzgerald doesn't know anything about it," objected Jim.

"No, but he will," said Campbell.

"Where's the gate?" asked Jim.

"Straight over the hill," said Campbell, waving his arm. "I left it open. Shut it when you go through."

Jim rode off at a trot. The dog's howls were unnerving him. I had to do it, he thought, but he felt rather sick.

When he got to the house it was necessary to ride across a piece of mown lawn in order to get to the kitchen window. But the ground was parched and the grass withered from the intense heat of August, so he didn't believe his riding on it was doing much harm.

Clara looked up startled. She had been washing dishes by an open window, and the sudden apparition of Jim on his horse made her throw up her hands dripping with suds.

"Lord, you scared me!" she said.

Jim delivered his message about calling the vet and the dog warden.

"What's wrong?" asked Clara.

"A dog bit one of the sheep," Jim informed her. It was hard for him to keep his voice from trembling.

"One of your dogs?" asked Clara suspiciously.

"No," replied Jim with indignation. "Campbell said to tell them Mr. Fitzgerald wants them to hurry." Abruptly, he turned and rode away so that she would stop asking questions and go to the telephone. What he really wanted was a drink of water.

He couldn't think of any reason for going back to the pasture, so he headed his horse in the direction of home. As soon as he was out of sight of the house, he dropped the reins on Warrior's neck and embraced him with both his arms. "You were great," he said. "Gosh, you were great. If you'd missed that jump, if you'd hit it just the least bit, we'd have turned right over. You're the best jumper in the world and I think your war-paint patches are beautiful. Anybody who says they're not, why, they're—why, they're *crazy*."

Taking advantage of the loose reins, Warrior grabbed for a bite of grass, and Jim let him get away with it. Right then, nothing was too good for his horse. As a matter of fact, he often felt sorry to make Warrior keep walking through a field of delicious grass or clover. It was a little like making a boy walk between tables spread with hamburgers and ice cream cones without even letting him take a bite. "Eat away. You deserve it," said Jim. But after a moment he pulled up Warrior's head and made him walk along.

As he rode into the dusky coolness of the woods,

thunder muttered with a sound like a wagon rattling over a loose plank bridge and finished with bumps like a hollow cask bouncing down a stony hillside. Then on the leafy ceiling above him, he heard a gentle pattering and felt the rain falling softly on his head and shoulders.

By the time he came within sight of the barn, the rain had begun to pour down in earnest. He had left his shirt on the fence, and his wet back felt cool. Rain ran down his hair and into his eyes, but he didn't hurry his horse along. Full of a sense of triumph, he was pretending he was an Indian chief returning from a war in which he had conquered his enemy and protected his territory.

Chapter 12

JIM LAY UNDER THE APPLE TREE BY THE KITCHEN window. He was trying hard to stop himself from thinking about the Hunter Trial in which he would be competing that afternoon. Flat on his back, he looked up through leaves translucent with sunlight and realized he was keeping so still that a bird hopping along a twig where a small green apple hung didn't even know he was there.

When the apples became ripe, in another month or so, his mother would make them into pies, brown Betty, apple dumplings, applesauce and other delicious desserts. The tree by the pasture gate he called Boots' Tree, although he, too, enjoyed eating the red apples. The one under which he was lying would have yellow apples in the fall; crisp, a little tart, and fine for cooking. He always thought of this as Mother's Tree.

He could hear her washing pots and pans in the sink, and he remembered how, in the spring, she loved to look out the window while she was working and enjoy the apple blossoms. In the autumn he could always count on her saying, "The golden apples of the Hesperides," as she looked at the tree. Once, he had asked her what she meant.

"It was a story in Greek mythology," she had replied, "but I don't remember what it was about. I like the sound of the words, that's all. They just describe this tree when the apples are all yellow and shining against a silver-blue sky."

His mother got a lot of pleasure out of skies and sunsets and flowers and things like that. She didn't seem to care that she didn't have jewelry and a fur coat and a lot of new dresses. Funny, thought Jim.

He lifted his right hand to see if there was any white paint under his fingernails. The movement frightened the bird and he flew away. Yes, there was still a little paint on his thumb, and he folded his fingers over to hide it thinking that if his mother noticed she would say, "It's a whole week since you painted that tack room. You can't be washing your hands very thoroughly." He began remembering in detail how nice the room looked with all the old harness cleared away and only his saddle and bridle left. The horse pictures he's been saving for years were thumbtacked to the walls and outlined with old Christmas ribbons so that they looked as if they were hanging in red frames on the white wall. The place now had a shipshape appearance, and he felt proud of the job he had done.

"Jim," his mother's voice came to him through the kitchen window. "Oh, Jim."

He closed his eyes. Probably she wanted him to do a job for her and he wasn't in the mood. If he kept quiet she wouldn't know he had heard.

The screen door banged. I guess she wanted me to get the mail, he thought. A moment before he had heard the mailman's car stopping by their box beside the road.

Presently, he opened one eye and saw her walking back toward the house sorting over the letters. Some would be orders for fertilizer, and these she would put on his father's desk in the living room.

Suddenly, she paused and looked about her, holding an envelope aloft. "Jim," she called loudly. "Jim, there's a letter for you."

How funny! he thought. Who's writing to me?

Catching sight of him lying under the tree, his mother started toward him as he rose to his feet.

The envelope she gave him was pale blue and he ripped it open.

"Who's it from?" asked his mother.

"Mrs. Fitzgerald," said Jim who, having glanced at the signature, had begun with intense concentration to read the letter.

"What does she say?" asked Mrs. Evans.

Jim folded the letter and put it in his pocket. His mother's eyes followed his movements, and he felt she would have liked to look at it herself.

"She wants me to come to tea in two weeks when

they get back from New York," said Jim. "She says they want to thank me for saving the sheep, and they want me to meet their son who's coming over from Paris."

"Well," said Mrs. Evans, "that's nice, I suppose. You deserve to be thanked for saving their sheep." But her brow was furrowed with lines of thought. "You know, Jim," she began impulsively, "there are a lot of rich families living around us, people who commute to their jobs, like Mr. Crofton, and wealthy, retired people like the Fitzgeralds. They have a lot of things we don't have, like big houses and people to work for them. I know you admire Mr. Crofton's cars. You seem to feel a shiny, new car about every year is terribly important. I've had the feeling for a long time that you were discontented with us and with the way we live and with your home." She hesitated and looked at him as if she realized she was failing to communicate to him something that was troubling her.

"Like, for example, Jim, when you came home after having tea with the Fitzgeralds, you seemed so critical of everything we have, and you said our house seemed so small."

"I think their house is great. Is there anything wrong with that?" asked Jim.

"No, of course not," said his mother. "But is that sort of thing really so important to you? I realize we live simply, compared to some of the people around here. But Dad and I are happy. And you used to be, too."

Jim gave her a sullen look. But his mother went on. "I know you wish we had a new car. And maybe we will, someday. But when you act so grumpy you . . ." His mother hesitated. "Well, you kind of spoil things for all of us."

"I'm going to give Warrior a little extra grooming," said Jim, starting to edge away. "Mr. Sheldon's picking him up at twelve o'clock."

"It's eleven-fifteen now," said his mother. "I've made some sandwiches. We can eat them in the car on the way over. Your father should be back soon. What time did you tell me your class was?"

"One-thirty," replied Jim. Just saying the words made his skin begin to prickle. The full impact of what this afternoon was going to mean of success or failure suddenly struck him, and he began to feel rather strange in the middle. It seemed as if a whole family of butterflies had found their way into his stomach. The thought of how he had practiced all these weeks to beat Tubby and that at last the day had arrived suddenly overwhelmed him.

Jim started working on the horse with his thoughts in a whirl. There was one thing he had not told his mother about Mrs. Fitzgerald's letter. *This is going to be a very special occasion, Jim,* she had written. What could the special part be, he wondered. Perhaps, thought Jim, I'm really related to them. He wanted so much to feel at home and part of the luxury of the big, stone house. If I lived there, he thought to himself, I'd walk through every room and explore and goodness knows what I might find. He began to wonder again about the thing they were going to tell him. Perhaps it was just that they wanted to adopt him. All the time he was having this wild daydream, he continued to work on his horse, going over his already shiny coat with a cloth, giving his mane and tail a final combing and laying it with a water brush.

When Mr. Sheldon arrived a little earlier than expected to pick Warrior up, the boy was ready for him. He had bandaged his horse's tail so he would not rub it on the tail gate of the truck, and had collected a bucket, a sponge, and a sweat scraper to use if the horse was very hot when he finished jumping.

Mr. Sheldon eyed the horse and the boy approvingly. "I was pleased when your father sent me that check and said you'd decided you wanted to keep him," he declared. "You have a great horse there. I suppose I should be sorry I let him go for what I did, but I like to see a horse and a boy or a girl really suited. You're getting on well with him, aren't you?"

"Yes, we get on fine," said Jim. "He hardly ever tries to buck now."

Mr. Sheldon nodded. "I wish that Crofton boy was doing as well with his horse as you are with yours. I sold him a well-schooled animal, but the boy's beginning to get refusals. He has hard hands and he won't let go enough so the horse can jump properly. He's always hauling on his mouth."

Barberry was already standing inside the van. He turned his head as far as the rope he was tied with would allow, in order to watch Warrior walk up the ramp and into the stall next to him.

"See you over there," said Mr. Sheldon. "Remember to move right along when you face that triple bar. Don't let him slow up."

Jim stood for a moment watching as they drove away. Those butterflies were flying around like crazy things inside his stomach. Maybe he'd better have a drink of water to quiet them down. The thought of a sandwich made him feel rather sick. His jodhpur boots needed a shine. Where had he left his hard cap?

"Gosh, I'd better hurry!" said Jim aloud, and he ran his tongue over his dry lips.

Chapter 13

"WHAT TIME IS IT?" ASKED JIM FOR THE FOURTH TIME in five minutes.

"It's thirteen to one," patiently replied his father, who had lifted his hand from the steering wheel to look at his watch. Then he glanced over his shoulder to the back seat and smiled at Jim who sat leaning forward, his whole attitude one of extreme tension.

"Simmer down," said Mr. Evans. "If you don't beat Tubby, it's not going to be the end of the world. I used to feel like you do now when our company was going to attack in Korea. I'd look at my watch and find only half a minute had passed since the last time I'd looked."

Jim had never heard his father talk much about his war experiences. They seemed to be something he wanted to forget.

Mrs. Evans was looking out the front seat window on her side of the car. She was wearing a pink dress, and her hair was neat and smooth. Jim had to admit that when she bothered to dress up she was a mother you could be proud of.

"Here we are," she cried. "There's a sign just ahead, see it? Hunter Trials."

The boy noticed a red arrow on a white sign pointing down a lane to the right. As they swung off the main road, they met up with a line of horse trailers and cars moving slowly through an open gate into a large field. Jim could see rail jumps and chicken coops marked with red flags and white. He was pleased to see that as he had expected, there was not one painted jump. The chicken coops were perhaps the easiest, being built just like a hen coop with sides running up to a ridge at the top. They made a horse take off better than the rail jumps.

Now the line of cars and horse vans was moving ahead and as Mr. Evans guided their car through the gate into the big field, Jim saw the triple bar, and his heart turned over. Warrior can do it, he thought. He can do it easily. Still, it was a formidable-looking obstacle.

In the crowd about him he sought a face he knew, but people stared back at him or didn't even give him a glance. So it was with a pleasant shock of recognition that he noticed Mr. Sheldon holding Warrior over by the refreshment tent. Nearby, Tubby was gathering up his reins and preparing to mount Barberry.

"I'll get out here," said Jim, starting to open the door of the slowly moving car.

"Have you a handkerchief?" asked his mother. "I

wish you'd eaten more than one sandwich. If you feel hungry there are lots left," and she patted the paper bag on her lap.

"I think we'll park right here and walk over to that hill slope where most of the people are sitting," said Mr. Evans, stopping the car. "If you want anything we'll be there." And he waved his hand to indicate a slope which commanded a view of all the jumps.

"Okay," answered Jim between tight lips.

"Relax," advised his father encouragingly. "This is supposed to be fun."

Fun, thought Jim. I wish it were over.

Although the day was ideally warm and sunny, although the people he passed were dressed in gay-colored clothes, although there was a nice smell of roasting hot dogs from the refreshment tent and a springy feel to the grass beneath his feet, still, to him, everything appeared hard and unkind and almost unreal, as if painted on pasteboard. For the hundredth time he licked his lips and the more he licked them the dryer they felt. Even his mouth felt dry.

"How's he feeling?" he asked, as he walked up to Mr. Sheldon holding Warrior.

"Full of beans," said the man. "We had a good trip over, no problems. I believe he could jump the moon. Just give him his head." Warrior's tail bandage had been removed by Mr. Sheldon. The horse looked sleek and fit and strong.

Jim tightened his girth, pulled down the stirrup irons, then gathered up his reins and mounted.

"Good luck," said Mr. Sheldon, patting Warrior's neck. "Tubby goes fourth and you go sixth. Try and cheer him up, he's having a bad case of the jitters. Show him the course. A map's posted over there on that oak tree," and he pointed in a straight line in front of him.

With leg pressures and reins, Jim guided Warrior to Tubby's side. "Hi," he said.

"Hi," answered Tubby. Then, automatically but in a shaky voice, Tubby began to boast. "My horse is out of a thoroughbred mare by an Arabian stallion. These jumps will just be cinchy for him."

Jim opened his mouth to say, "Arabians aren't usually very good jumpers," but suddenly he looked at Tubby and decided not to say anything. The boy's face was the color of an underdone milk pudding, and his eyes looked like raisins that had sunk during the cooking. Poor Tubby, thought Jim, he's absolutely petrified, and for the first time he felt no inclination to make a sharp retort.

They walked their horses along side by side. Jim glanced once more at the pale face beside him. All his boasting, he thought, is only because he knows he isn't so great. His father's awful to him. Why, he doesn't even act as if he liked him. All Tubby's got is his ancestors and the expensive things his family give him. He doesn't look a bit like his mother or father. Maybe long ago there was a grandfather or an uncle who was fat and dumpy. He tried to remember what he had been told about genes.

"Where are you going?" asked Tubby.

"Look, this shows us the course," said Jim, stopping beside the oak tree. They waited for a girl mounted on a blue roan mare to move away and then they rode their horses close enough to see.

"It's easy," said Jim. "You just keep riding in a circle except for that post-and-rail where you have to cut out to the left and then go back over a ditch before taking the triple bar."

"We'd better trot," exclaimed Tubby abruptly. "The first horse in our class is being called. Hear it?"

"Okay. I want to warm up too," said Jim. "I'll watch you start later. I want to speak to Mom and Dad."

Somewhere over on the hill slope among all those people sitting on the grass he knew he would find his family. So he jogged along, with Warrior taking a hold on the bit, his neck arched, wanting to move on faster. Jim kept his eyes open until he saw his mother's pink dress and his father's plaid sport shirt.

Both of them rose to their feet as he neared them and moved eagerly toward him as if they wanted to help. In their eyes he saw a smiling pride as they looked up at him on his horse.

"Can I have some money for a Coke?" asked Jim.

"Sure," agreed his father, reaching quickly into his pocket. "Here's a quarter. Do you really want to drink it before you ride?"

"No, afterward," said Jim. He was looking about him and realizing that this area certainly was the vantage point from which one could see all of the jumps. The horse that was on course had just refused the second chicken coop. I think I'll watch Tubby from here, he decided.

His parents looked as though they would like him to stick around and talk to them, but he knew he must warm Warrior up some more.

"I'll see you," he said, and, squeezing his legs against his horse's sides, he made him walk forward.

Now that he was mounted he felt a hundred times better. The familiar neck and pricked ears in front of him, the comfortable creak of his saddle, the way his legs fitted so naturally to the horse's sides, all taken together made him relax.

Warrior was acting springy and right up on his toes as Jim cantered him around. He shied playfully at a woman carrying a paper bag and pretended to be much more astonished than he really was. It must be getting near the time for Tubby to go in, thought Jim finally, and the idea occurred to him that he'd like to see how his rival was feeling now.

Right by the starting line he found Barberry with Tubby hunched on his back. Mr. Crofton stood beside the horse's head delivering a lecture. Jim heard him say, "I didn't buy you an expensive horse just so you'd chicken out at the last minute and say, 'I don't want to ride, these jumps are too big.' " Mr. Crofton had imitated a whining voice. "You buck up and go in there and do your stuff," he said. "There's a good-looking cup that goes to the winner of this class and I want to take it home with us."

Tubby's lower lip was trembling, and Jim feared he might be going to cry. Impulsively he said, "Hey listen Tubby, take the triple bar good and fast. Don't let him slow up."

The fat face turned and looked at him, and a shrewd look came into the raisin-brown eyes. Just then the announcer called, "The fourth competitor is Barberry, ridden by Thomas Crofton." Jim smiled. It was funny to hear Tubby called Thomas. Turning Warrior, he rode off quickly so as to be in a position to view the course. As he pulled to a stop on the high part of the slope, he saw Tubby take the first jump. The horse certainly wasn't going as well as he had been when the Croftons first bought him. Tubby was hanging onto his mouth and Barberry fought to get his head. However, being a willing jumper and hard to discourage, he kept going in spite of the boy's bad riding. They had one refusal at a chicken coop, and Jim felt his heart leap with unholy joy. Now he saw horse and rider take a small post-and-rail, then clear the ditch and head for the triple bar. And Tubby began to slow Barberry up. Really slow him up.

What's he doing? thought Jim wildly. Then the truth dawned on him. Tubby was doing exactly what Jim had told him *not* to do. "Oh, gosh!" muttered Jim. "He thought I was giving him bad advice when I told him to go fast. He thought I wanted to make him lose."

Surely Barberry would refuse. It was obvious he

couldn't make it going at that pace. But to Jim's horror, he saw the horse take off and make a try at jumping the three bars.

For one breathtaking moment Barberry was in the air. Then he landed way short, right in the middle of the jump and turned over, falling, legs up. Jim gasped. It looked to him as though the horse had landed right on top of Tubby, who had been flung to the ground as the horse fell. Tubby's body was completely hidden by Barberry who was attempting to struggle to his feet. Jim thought of how fat and squashy Tubby was. He felt sick.

The spectators were quiet as though struck dumb by the sight. The announcer's voice broke stridently over

the loudspeaker. "A doctor is needed at the tenth jump. Send the ambulance to the tenth jump."

Lurching out over the field came a long, white car with a red cross painted on the window. Someone was running ahead carrying a black bag. The spectators on the hill slope rose to their feet. The running man seemed to have triggered a mob response, and people took a few first steps starting to run toward the accident.

Suddenly, a commanding figure faced the crowd and held up his hand. Jim saw with amazement that it was his father. "Stay back! Don't move!" he ordered. "No one is to go down there." The surging crowd stopped at the voice of authority. "The next horse will be going soon. Keep your seats," directed Mr. Evans, and the crowd sat down.

Jim looked with awe at his father. He had spoken like a general to an army. Below him, he saw that Barberry had regained his feet and was being led away. A stretcher had been laid on the ground and Tubby's still form was being gently placed upon it. Jim strained his eyes to see blood, he felt sick and curious at the same time.

Fascinated, he watched two men lift the stretcher carefully and shove it into the ambulance. Tubby's mother and father were helped in, then the door was closed. Slowly, the ambulance moved away, swaying over the rough ground.

Jim closed his mouth which had been hanging open. He sat up straight in his saddle. With a sudden instinct, he knew that his father would be looking for him, but he didn't want to talk. He must go in there and ride. All at once, he wanted to be like his father, whom he could imagine carrying on in battle even though he had just seen someone blown up beside him.

Jim saw that the horse that was to go just before him was on course. Apparently it hadn't taken long to mend the broken fence. Jim's number was being called now. "Number Six, please be ready to start."

He trotted Warrior across the meadow grass and drew to a halt near a man with a stopwatch.

But the starter appeared to be so busy reading his watch that when he glanced up he had a glazed, expressionless look on his face. A woman in a yellow dress standing near him gave Jim a smile which at that moment he felt unable to return.

It wasn't long before the girl on the blue roan came walking back. She must have had three refusals at some fence and been disqualified.

"All right, Number Six, one minute to go," said the starter, glancing at his watch and then looking at Jim. The boy walked Warrior in a big circle as the count went on. Thirty seconds to go. Fifteen seconds. Ten seconds. Five—four—three—two—one. Go!

And Jim was away toward the first obstacle, a chicken coop with its waving marker flags, the red on the right, the white on the left. And he was over! He could feel joy in the horse as he jumped. All Jim's nervousness had vanished and he responded to the thrill of galloping hoofs carrying him across the wide meadow toward the next jump, which was a post-and-rails. Up and over! And again away and on toward the next obstacle.

Almost before he knew it he was crossing the ditch that came just before the triple bar. There before him loomed the sinister jump that had been Tubby's downfall.

Squeezing with his legs, he quickened Warrior's pace and rode him at the obstacle with a will, throwing his heart over, knowing the horse must do it, sure he could do it.

Warrior, with forward-pricked ears, assessed what lay before him and took off far enough back to carry them in one tremendous leap safely to the other side. As he landed he celebrated his feat with a lighthearted bounce that nearly unseated Jim. But not quite. And then away they went and sailed the last three jumps easily. Jim really let him out over the finish line and they pounded across, with Warrior's ears flat back. Jim was smiling broadly and feeling that this was the nicest bit of country he had ever ridden over and that the whole world was his friend.

Slowly easing Warrior to a stop, he found himself near the woman in yellow. "Well ridden," she cried enthusiastically.

Jim was about to dismount and take care of his horse when a man with a Polaroid camera snapped his picture. "That's a great jumper you have there," said the man, smiling broadly. "I like his markings too. Very striking. This will make a good picture. Your blue shirt gives just the right accent to the brown and white horse. I'll give you a picture if you don't mind posing again." He pulled out the first picture, looked at it, nodded, and holding up his camera, snapped once more. Then he handed a photograph to Jim. The boy thanked him, pleased to have a picture of Warrior for his tack room. He felt all aglow with satisfaction. The picture was great. It showed Warrior with his head up, his ears pricked, and looking as if he could do the whole course again without any trouble. Jim also rather liked the way he himself appeared. He was sitting straight, his legs firmly against the horse's sides, his heels down, his reins held easily but ready to check any sudden movement on the part of his horse. Beaming with pride, he looked up and saw Mr. Sheldon walking toward him, his face worried and distressed. "Hard luck, Jim," he said. "You're disqualified. You missed the little post-and-rail just before the ditch."

"Oh, no!" cried Jim aghast. Then he remembered. Yes, it was true, he'd forgotten to swing left. And after having pointed it out to Tubby and told him what they should do! What a fool he was! Dismounting, he ran up his irons and eased Warrior's girth by a couple of holes. He wanted to give him a drink, but he knew he mustn't. Not until he'd cooled him off.

"You'd have won otherwise," said Mr. Sheldon.

"Warrior did so well and I let him down," said Jim in an agonized voice.

"He went wonderfully for you. You have a terrific

horse there. Don't worry, you'll have plenty more chances," said the man. "The thing that upsets me is that I didn't warn Tubby to take that triple bar fast."

"I told him," said Jim, "but he wouldn't listen to me. Do you know if he is . . ." Jim hesitated. "Is he hurt very badly?"

"A call came just a minute ago from the hospital saying that both his legs are broken and so is his collarbone. But they don't think he has any internal injuries. He especially wants to see you."

"See *me*?" echoed Jim. "What does he want to see me for?"

Chapter 14

"Do I *have* to go to the hospital and see Tubby?" asked Jim the next morning at breakfast.

"No, of course you don't *have* to," said Mr. Evans, "but I think you should if he's asked to see you."

"He's not my friend. We don't like each other much," said Jim. For a moment he reflected while he buttered a hot muffin. Then he asked, "If someone in your platoon, someone you didn't really like, got wounded, would you go to see him in the hospital?"

"If he wanted to see me, yes," answered Mr. Evans.

Jim sighed. "What time can you take me?"

"As soon as I finish writing a letter I've got to send off, then we'll go," said his father.

When Jim finished his breakfast, he went out to the barn to check on Warrior. The horse appeared glad to see him and nuzzled at his shoulder.

"Gosh, I'm sorry I let you down yesterday," he told him, stroking his warm, satiny neck. The memory of what his father had said came back to comfort him a little. Shortly after Jim had dismounted while he was leading his horse around in a circle to cool him off, his mother and father had come hurrying up to him.

"Jim," Mr. Evans had said, "I'm proud of you. I know you missed a jump, but you rode well. It took a lot of courage to face that triple bar and really want to take it after seeing what happened to Tubby. Everyone who was watching, at least those that I talked to afterward, said you rode at it in a way that made your horse know you wanted to go on. Mr. Sheldon told me a horse can sense the feelings of a rider and often refuses at a fence because he can tell the person on his back subconsciously hopes to stop and not have to take a jump he's scared of."

Remembering his father's words made Jim feel a little better. "Next time, Warrior," he said, "I'll keep my wits about me and we'll win. Do you forgive me for being a jerk?"

The horse nibbled playfully at the cloth of his shirt. "Are you saying you do," asked Jim, "or do you just want something to eat? Come on!" he declared impulsively. "I'll get you what you like."

A lead rope hung on a hook outside the stall and he snapped it onto the horse's halter then swung open the door, and they walked out of the dusky barn into the sunny day.

As they wandered along together, Warrior tried to drop his head to snatch at grass.

"No, no," said Jim. "Come on. I'll give you something better than that to eat."

Stopping beside the vegetable garden, he pulled a carrot from the moist earth and wiped it on the long grass. An old wooden tub was catching the drip from a spigot, to which a hose often was attached for watering the garden. Jim dipped the carrot up and down in the water until it came out clean and shiny, orange colored. The green tail of ferny leaves waggled as he bit on the root end just to see how it was going to taste. Then he handed it to Warrior who was bumping his head impatiently against his shoulder.

"Pretty good, isn't it?" asked Jim, stroking the horse's neck while he crunched away.

After a few minutes he said, "Let's go say hello to the beagles. Then I've got to put you back in the barn because I'm going to the hospital to see Tubby."

It never seemed strange to him that he talked to Warrior as if he understood everything he said. Mr. Sheldon had once told him about a girl who talked to her horse. All the time she was riding him she chattered away because otherwise, being very scared, she held her breath, which made her feel faint. To Jim, that seemed a silly reason to talk to a horse. She could have recited the alphabet just as well.

He started to lead Warrior toward the kennel, but the horse laid back his ears and jerked his head toward the row of carrots. "Oh, so you're telling me you want another. Okay. Just because you were such a good boy yesterday, you may have one more." He leaned over and hauled at the thickest carrot top he could find. Up came a fat beauty that he washed in the tub before presenting it to his horse. Eagerly reaching with his head, Warrior took the carrot in two bites. "Come on, you can chew while you walk," he said, and he led him toward the kennel where a great racket began as soon as the little hounds saw them.

Tigger, Tugger, Penny, and Lucy sprang against the wire of their enclosure and begged to be let out, panting and yelping eagerly.

"Look, I can't do it now," explained Jim in an earnest voice. "But I'll take you for a ride this afternoon."

"Ready to go, Jim?" called his father from the back porch of the house.

"I'll be there in just a second," shouted Jim.

When he came out of the barn after putting Warrior in his stall, he found his father waiting in the car. They settled down side by side for the ride into town.

"How did you make those people sit down again when they started to run?" asked Jim.

"It makes me boil when people run to look at an accident. The person who is hurt has enough trouble without having to endure a lot of curious ghouls peering down at him," said Mr. Evans.

Jim knew his father hadn't answered the question. Maybe he had learned to command people when he was a soldier. Jim guessed that must be it. He glanced at his father and felt proud of him—even though they were riding in old Finny.

"Are you going to go with me when I see Tubby?" asked Jim.

"No. I'll just wait down by the information desk," said Mr. Evans. "I'm not the one Tubby wants to see."

When they left their car in the hospital parking lot, Jim was sorry he'd ever agreed to make this visit. The tall building toward which they walked filled him with uneasiness as he imagined the aches and pains and fevers being cared for behind those walls and windows. He hoped he wouldn't hear any horrible groans or see anyone who had just been brought in from an automobile accident with his head cut off. Instinctively, he walked very close to his father who, he was sure, had seen so much blood and mess in the war that this was nothing to him.

They entered by a big glass door and Jim followed his father to the reception desk where a young woman in white thumbed through a file when Mr. Evans asked to see Thomas Crofton.

"Third floor, Room 315. Go straight ahead and turn right to find the elevator," said the woman in white, handing out a card. "He's only allowed one visitor at a time," she announced briskly, and turned to an old woman in a droopy hat who was asking to see her husband.

"Hey, can't you go up with me?" whispered Jim.

"You can do it by yourself," said his father. "We'll go together to the elevator. Get off at the third floor and look for Room 315. If anyone stops you, show them this," and he handed Jim the piece of blue cardboard with something printed on it.

Now they were standing by the closed doors to the elevator. A young doctor dressed all in white with a stethoscope hanging around his neck, who was standing there also, pressed a button. Then they all waited.

A nurse in a white cap and blue striped uniform trundled up a stand on wheels that carried some grisly looking bottles with strange-appearing mixtures in them.

Jim didn't like the thought of parting with his father. He felt awed by this unfamiliar environment; small and lost in the great white corridor where any one of the closed doors might open into an operating room or the morgue.

The elevator door slid silently open, the nurse and the doctor walked into the yawning cavern. Jim saw a white stretcher on wheels already inside. Thank heaven no one was on it.

"I'll meet you right here in fifteen minutes," said his father, and he smiled encouragingly as Jim walked into the elevator and the doors closed.

Slowly, they ascended. No one said anything. The nurse and the doctor got off at the second floor.

Jim pressed the button marked 3 and up he went. The elevator eased to a stop, the doors slid silently open, and he walked off hastily before they could close again.

A pretty nurse dressed all in white who was passing by with a tray of medicine smiled at him and asked, "Looking for somebody?" In appearance, she was rather like his mother, only a little younger. He ventured a timid smile. "I want Room 315," he said. "I've come to see Tubby Crofton."

"I've just been giving him his medicine," said the nurse, in the tone of voice she would have used if she had said, "I've just been giving him a vanilla ice cream cone."

Smiling, she pointed to a door on which Jim saw the number 315 painted in black.

"Thanks," mumbled Jim.

"Don't stay too long," said the nurse cheerfully. "He's pretty uncomfortable today, but he'll be feeling better tomorrow. Are you by chance Jim Evans?" she asked.

Jim nodded.

"He began asking for you the minute he came out of the anesthetic after having his legs set. I know he'll be glad to see you." Giving him another smile, she hurried away down the corridor.

Jim walked hesitantly toward the half-open door. "Hey, Tubby," he said softly, giving a light tap.

"Come in," said Tubby in a loud voice.

Reassured, Jim walked into the room and saw lying on the white bed a form whose two legs encased in casts and bandages were raised into the air on ropes and pulleys. But flat on the pillow lay Tubby's familiar face, turned to look sideways at him over a bandaged shoulder.

"Hi. How are you?" asked Jim.

"Not too bad," said Tubby cheerfully. "I broke my

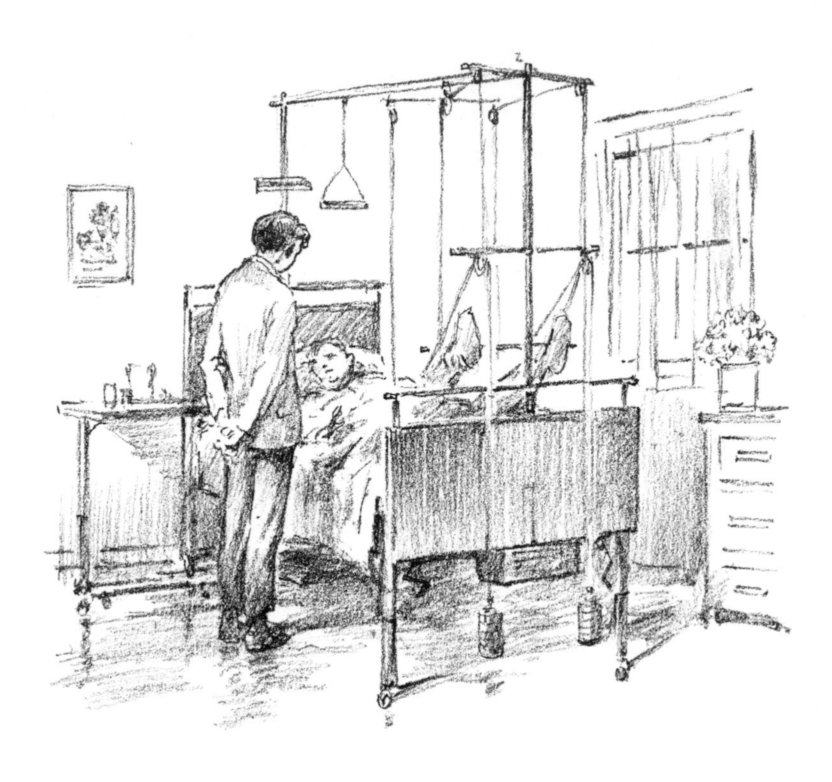

shoulder when I fell and then Barberry fell on my legs."

"Did it hurt?" asked Jim.

"You bet," said Tubby. "I'll say it did. But I was knocked out. I was unconscious until I got to the hospital." In his voice there was a note of pride in telling all he had been through.

"Gee," said Jim. "When can you ride again?"

Tubby's face twisted into an expression of dismay. "I don't think I want to ride anymore," he said. "I think maybe I'd like to play tennis."

"Tennis!" said Jim scornfully.

"Hey, Jim," said Tubby, "you know something

funny? I thought you were telling me to go fast because you wanted me to fall so you'd win. Someone told Dad when they were picking me up that if I'd only gone faster, I'd have been all right."

"Yes, I guess you would have," admitted Jim. "Anyhow, Barberry's learned not to try to jump when he knows he can't make it."

"You can practice on our painted jumps," said Tubby.

"Thanks," said Jim.

"Anytime," said Tubby.

"What's it like being here?" asked Jim.

"Not bad," said Tubby. "They're real nice to me. Only they won't give me a candy bar. The doctor is a great guy. He said I was a good patient," he added with pride.

"I guess I'd better be going," said Jim.

"Stick around," said Tubby.

"No, I have to meet my father," said Jim. He looked at Tubby's face on the pillow. "When you're all well we can ride together," he said. "We'll go nice and easy. You won't have to jump if you don't want to."

A look of gratitude at being understood came into Tubby's eyes.

"Thanks for coming to see me," he said.

"So long," said Jim. As he started to go out of the room, a large man in a dark suit was coming in. He's probably Tubby's doctor, thought Jim, as he edged sideways to let the man pass.

"Been visiting Thomas?" boomed the doctor.

"Yes, sir," said Jim.

Now that it was over, he was glad he'd done it. For some reason he felt sort of warm and happy. And he could hardly wait to get back to Warrior who had carried him safely over the triple bar.

Chapter 15

It was a glorious, fresh, cool morning radiant with September sunshine. The whole world seemed to be singing with exciting possibilities. Jim didn't know how he could wait until it was time to saddle his horse, ride through the woods, then over the fields and up the hill to have tea with the Fitzgeralds.

Killing time, he wandered aimlessly about the place. A peach tree grew near the back porch and he selected a ripe and downy fruit. Through the tender skin, he smelled sun-warmed lusciousness even before he bit into it. Juice ran down his chin as he strolled about, eating with sucking bites.

Last year, near the vegetable garden, his father had planted a Concord grapevine. The bunches were only green bullets now, but he could envision how blue and plump they would be in October. He imagined himself pressing a grape against his mouth and how the slippery fruit would pop out of its skin and slide between his teeth and down his throat. Carelessly, he threw away the peach pit. His hands were sticky, so he dipped them in the wooden tub by the vegetable garden and wiped juice from his mouth with his wet fingers.

There were still a few carrots left in the garden, and he decided to take one to Warrior who was turned out for the morning in the pasture. Grabbing a ferny carrot top, he gave a good pull, but it broke off in his hands. So did the second and the third.

"Heck," said Jim, "the ground's too hard. I'll have to get a spade."

He went back to the house and found his mother sitting on the porch. Her face was flushed. "I've been canning tomatoes and I felt so warm in the kitchen I thought I'd cool off a minute," she said.

"Where's Dad's spade?" asked Jim.

"Down cellar, I think," said his mother. "He's put the tools away now that we're through gardening."

Jim went in the side door and down the cellar stairs. It was quiet here without the sound of puppies squeaking for food. The spade was leaning against the far wall where Lucy's pen had been. Jim brought it up with him and found his mother still sitting, her hands folded quietly in her lap, looking at the apple tree heavy with golden fruit.

"Will you help me prop up that branch, Jim?" she asked. "I'm afraid it's going to break." And she motioned toward fruit and leaves that hung so low they touched the grass.

"Sometime," said Jim. "I'm busy now." He walked away quickly before his mother could make up her mind to call him back. Carrying the spade he went to the garden where he dug the three carrots, bringing them up in lumps of earth. Propping the spade against the tub of water, he washed them after first cleaning off a little earth with his hands.

Then, holding the wet carrots he walked to the pasture gate.

"Come on, Warrior," he said to his horse who had already started moving toward him. "Here's something you like."

As the horse crunched away on the carrots, Jim said, "I'm going to take you in now and give you a good grooming. We're invited out to tea. I guess Campbell will give you a snack while I'm in the house."

After leading the horse into the shadowy barn where only a little sunlight filtered through the dusty windows, he crosstied him with ropes snapped to both sides of his halter.

Whistling cheerfully, Jim went into the tack room and picked up his grooming kit. But he stood a moment looking about admiringly at the paint job he had done and at his picture gallery. The photograph of Warrior made a fine addition. He had framed it in yellow ribbon so that it would stand out with special importance. He thought that the yellow frame set off the brown and white of Warrior's patches and his own blue shirt. One of the thumbtacks holding the ribbon had come loose, and he pushed it firmly back into the wall. Continuing his whistling, he went back to his horse, carrying the grooming kit.

"Now, Warrior, I'm going to give you the best grooming you ever had," he told him. "Today's a special day. I don't know just what's going to happen, but I think it's something wonderful," said Jim.

Picking up the horse's feet one after the other, he cleaned them out with a hoof pick. From the grooming kit box he next took the rubber currycomb. Holding it with the strap over his hand, he rubbed the horse's coat with a circular motion to take off any mud that had collected from his rolling in the pasture. Frequently, Jim knocked the currycomb against the stall door nearest him to dislodge the dirt.

After a while, he picked up the body brush and leaned his weight on it as he swept it over the horse's coat. From time to time, he cleaned the brush on the currycomb and then tapped the currycomb on the stall door.

Warrior enjoyed all the attention. Even when Jim combed his tail, he stood still. But by the time the boy got to his mane, he began to get a little restless and pawed the ground a few times and moved forward a step until the ropes fastened to his halter checked him.

"Nearly finished," said Jim, as he went over the mane and tail with a water brush and made them lie smooth. Mustn't forget to wash his hoofs, thought the boy, who by now was breathing hard from his efforts. Oh, but first I'd better sponge out his nostrils and wipe his eyes, ears, and dock.

At last he was ready for the final touches and, picking up a cloth, he rubbed the horse's coat until it shone a satiny brown and white.

Before putting him into his stall, he forked out some manure mixed with straw and dropped it into a wheelbarrow. He had learned the hard way by having to wash the horse's white legs with soap and water, that it saved time to keep his stall clean.

Checking on the water bucket, he found that it was full. "Good-by, Warrior," said Jim. "See you later." As he walked back toward the house he thought about the Croftons having a man who did all the stable chores. Jim didn't think he'd like that. Taking care of Warrior made him feel he knew the horse, and he was sure he could ride him all the better for that knowledge. When he finished grooming him he took great pride in the way his horse looked.

"Ready to eat, Jim?" asked his mother as he came into the kitchen where rows of glass jars filled with canned tomatoes stood on a shelf. "Your father called and said he's going to be late for lunch. I'll just save him some, and I think I'll wait and eat with him. Want to take yours out on the porch?"

"Sure," said Jim.

"Wash your hands," said his mother. "You're always forgetting to wash your hands before meals."

"Oh, gosh, do I have to?" asked Jim. But knowing what the answer would be, he was already on the way to do what she'd asked.

When he returned to the porch he sat down on the top step. In a moment his mother brought out a plate of golden waffles awash with melted butter and maple syrup. Crisp curls of bacon surrounded all this lusciousness and as she gave him the plate she also handed him a glass of cold milk.

"Thanks, Mom," he said, and noticed her face looked tired.

A nice breeze reached him here on the porch. In fact, it was almost too cool unless he sat in direct sunlight. So he shifted a few feet to the left to get out of the shadow.

Inside the house his mother had turned on the radio to an FM station that played classical music. She always did that while she worked. He thought what he was listening to was something called *The Pastoral Symphony*. Anyway, he liked it.

With his fork, he wiped a remaining fragment of waffle around the plate to absorb the last of the syrup and butter. Then he leaned back against a post supporting the porch roof and listened to the music.

Out of a corner of his eye he could see the apple tree. The branches nodding in the breeze appeared to him like arms conducting the rhythm of the symphony. The fluttering leaves moved as rapidly as fingers on a clarinet or flute. The tree seemed alive to the music. He closed his eyes. When he opened them there was silence and he realized he must have been sound asleep for some time.

He heard the screen door open and his mother came out. "Jim," she said, "I'm worried about your father. He isn't home yet. He's never as late as this."

Blinking his eyes, Jim yawned. "Oh, I guess he'll be here pretty soon," he said.

"Well, I feel anxious about him," said Mrs. Evans.

"What time is it?" asked Jim.

"It's two-thirty," said his mother.

"He'll be along," said Jim. "I think he said he was going to that big farm that has five hundred acres to try to sell them fertilizer. Probably they take a long time to persuade. I've got to saddle up and get going."

His tack had been well polished, and he saddled his horse feeling a sense of satisfaction at how nice everything looked.

Sad as it seemed, he recognized the necessity of disappointing the beagles, who were not allowed out alone because they ran away after rabbits and who looked to him for their exercise. But he just couldn't take them along. Four dogs romping with Master Toots and skidding on the Oriental rugs would not, he was sure, amuse the Fitzgeralds. He had taken the little hounds on a good ride yesterday but as he guided Warrior away from the barn he heard their frantic yelps.

Realizing he had started in plenty of time, he went a roundabout way and cantered along through fields where goldenrod was just beginning to turn a brassy yellow. All about him sounded the noisy chirr of cicadas and the cheep of crickets telling him, as they always did at this time of year, that autumn was just around the corner.

He passed by a pond and heard the glump of a bullfrog hiding in the reeds and cattails. "Do you want a drink, Warrior?" Jim asked, thinking to give him a couple of swallows. But when he took him to the edge of the pond, he only blew on the water.

"Well, come on," he said finally. "We've ridden more than an hour. Even if we're a little early, let's get on up there. We'll walk all the way to cool you off."

Once more they climbed the hill to what Jim had often thought of as the castle above the lake. Today, the sheep were pastured near the house, and he saw them peacefully grazing. Late roses bloomed in the garden, and recent rains had brought back an emerald greenness to the lawn that had hung on by its roots to life all through the parching heat of August.

At the stable he found Campbell, who took Warrior from him. The man was beaming.

"They have a nice surprise for you," he said.

"What?" asked Jim, wanting to get the suspense over.

"Oh, I'd better not give it away," said Campbell. "If I told you, then it wouldn't be a surprise."

Chapter 16

JIM WALKED TOWARD THE HOUSE AND AS HE WALKED he glanced down at his shirt which he was sorry to notice wasn't very clean. Furtively, he inspected his fingernails and then tried to remove traces of grime by picking at his left hand with his right thumbnail and vice versa. He had spent a lot of time grooming his horse, but, unfortunately, he had forgotten about his own appearance. The realization came to him that he must always have relied on his mother to pester him about being neat and clean, but today she had been busy worrying about his father and hadn't noticed how he looked. I'm not *too* bad, he thought, remembering that he had put on a clean shirt that morning. With an anxious gesture, he ran a hand over his hair to smooth it down.

Clara opened the door as soon as he rang. It seemed almost as if she'd been waiting for him.

"So the hero's coming to tea," she said. "You didn't

tell me that day when you scared me half to death at the kitchen window what it was you'd done."

She led the way through the hall and through the large drawing room to the small sitting room. Here, as before, he found Mr. and Mrs. Fitzgerald and Master Toots.

"Jim!" cried Mrs. Fitzgerald from her seat on the sofa behind the tea tray. "Come here, I want to thank you for saving our poor helpless sheep." Obediently, he went over and took her hand. She held his a moment and looked up at him gratefully.

"You did a good job," agreed Mr. Fitzgerald who was standing by the window. He reached a hand into his pocket.

"Not now," cried his wife. "Don't give it to him yet. Let's wait until Robert comes in. We found something for you in New York," she explained. "We hope you'll like it. We want you to know how much we appreciate the risk you took to save our sheep."

At that moment Clara brought in the tea pot and hot water kettle and set them on the tray in front of Mrs. Fitzgerald who lit the spirit lamp with a match from a small box that had been lying on the table next to her. Jim noticed her white, heavily ringed fingers. He remembered his mother's hands, rough and sometimes red from all the work she did in the house and the garden, work she appeared to enjoy so much.

The heat of the blue flame made the hot water kettle, suspended above it, begin to hum, and Mrs. Fitzgerald fussed with the tea cups, setting them here and there on the tray.

Master Toots, after a brief greeting when Jim arrived, had returned to curl up in an easy chair. The boy was shocked to see the roly-poly form the beagle had acquired from all the feeding and pampering he had received. Eyes closed, he was breathing like an asthmatic pug. You sure couldn't hunt rabbits, thought Jim. You'd fall over in a fit after running two yards.

Clara brought in sandwiches and cakes and set them on a three-tiered stand near the tea table.

"Are you hungry, Jim?" asked Mrs. Fitzgerald. "Let me give you your tea now." She poured a cup then put in the two lumps and the cream Jim had said he liked. "Robert should be here any minute," she added with a bright hopefulness.

Mr. Fitzgerald grunted, and Jim sensed again that the father disapproved of his son, while Mrs. Fitzgerald tried to defend him.

"Will you have your tea?" she asked her husband, who had remained standing by the window.

"Late as usual, holding everything up," said Mr. Fitzgerald irritably. "That's the way he's always been."

"Robert's out shooting squirrels," explained Mrs. Fitzgerald. "Help yourself to the sandwiches, Jim. You must be hungry after your ride."

"When he visits us, Robert always loves to walk about with a gun," she went on. "Last year he was here much later in the season and I tell you, we had some fine roast pheasants. Clara hates to pluck off the feathers though, and I'm certain she'd never skin a squirrel. Don't wait for him, dear. Have your tea," urged Mrs. Fitzgerald, and she poured a cup and put in a slice of lemon. "Take this to Mr. Fitzgerald, will you, please, Jim?"

Obediently, the boy set aside his own cup and the sandwich he was eating and rose from his chair to receive the cup from her hand. Walking carefully so as not to slop any tea in the saucer, he made his way around the table and offered the cup to Mr. Fitzgerald who had remained standing by the window.

The old man took the cup and at the same moment exclaimed. "There he is!"

Walking across the lawn toward the house Jim saw a man, a man dressed in a red shooting jacket. He had a black moustache and on his head was an odd-shaped, black hat rather like a pixie's. A never-to-be-forgotten scene flashed before Jim's eyes. He imagined he again heard the shot, saw Boots lying bleeding on the ground, and this very figure turning and fleeing from what he had done, away into the woods.

Jim clutched at one of the heavy curtains and with the other hand he pointed toward the lawn. "Who's that?" he breathed.

Mr. Fitzgerald looked at Jim's ashen face. Then in a hearty voice meant to be reassuring he said, "Why, that's Robert. Who did you think he was, a robber? Haven't you ever seen a man with a gun before?"

"I have to go," gasped Jim. "I have to go right now."

"Why, Jim, what's the matter?" exclaimed Mrs. Fitzgerald. "Don't you feel well?"

But the boy, behaving like someone trapped, was plunging toward the door of the sitting room. "I'm sorry, I can't stay any longer," he said breathlessly. "My mother needs me, the apple tree, Dad's not home." He hurried through the great drawing room and on into the hall, skidding on the edges of Oriental rugs and bumping into chairs as he fled.

As he was reaching for the handle of the heavy front door, it slowly opened. Still wearing the black pixie hat, still carrying the gun, Robert walked into the shadowy hall.

Jim leaped back a step. Then with the swiftness of a cornered animal, he dodged around the sinister figure, brushing against the red shooting jacket as he dove past and on out the front door into the light and sunshine.

Outside, he glanced back over his shoulder after going a few yards, but saw only the blank windows of the house staring at him—no one was following.

Panting, he slowed down and began to walk. His thoughts flashed to his mother and his father and his home, and he wanted to get back to them as soon as possible. Why had his father been so late for lunch? Had he been in an accident? Jim remembered with shame having ridden away leaving his mother alone and worried. Maybe the limb of the apple tree had broken from the weight of all the fruit that was bearing it down while he'd been gone. And he'd said he was too busy to help prop it up!

Suddenly all the grandeur of the Fitzgeralds' house bored him. The tack room he had painted and fixed up himself seemed to him far more interesting than the finest room in the great stone house. How stupid I've been! he thought. I've already got everything I really want. I've got a horse to ride and dogs to play with and parents who love me, and what have I been doing? Having crazy daydreams about being the son of the man who killed Boots and ran away. Now, with all his heart he wanted to see his father. He felt frantic to get home and find out that both his parents were all right.

Campbell was standing in the stable door smoking his short pipe.

As Jim hurried toward him, he said, "Well, you didn't stay long. Let's see the gold watch."

"Gold watch?" repeated Jim, stupidly.

"Yes," replied Campbell. "The watch they bought you in New York. The surprise."

"Oh," said Jim, "I didn't wait. I have to get home right away. I think something may have happened to my father."

Campbell knocked out his pipe on the heel of his boot and hurried to help Jim saddle up. "Did your mother telephone?" he asked.

"No," said Jim. "I'll explain sometime. I've got to hurry. Thanks for everything," and he swung onto Warrior's back.

The minute they came to the bottom of the steep hill, he put his horse into a fast trot. As he posted along, he prayed. "Oh, God, please don't let anything have happened to Dad.

"And the apple tree, don't let the apple tree be broken. It would be all my fault and Mom loves it so."

As he came in sight of his house, he strained his eyes to see Finny parked by the barn, which would mean his father was home. Instead, he saw a shiny new red station wagon standing by the back door. He felt sick. A doctor, he thought. Dad's hurt. He put Warrior into a canter.

The sound of pounding hoofs brought his mother to the door. As he drew to a halt beside the porch, she ran forward exclaiming, "What's happened, Jim?"

"Where's Dad?" he cried, his face full of anxiety and distress.

At that moment his father, looking his usual self, came out through the door. "Who do you think you are, Paul Revere? What's going on?" he asked.

"Dad, are you all right? Where's Finny?" gasped Jim.

"Poor Finny," said his father. "She gave up the ghost on a back road miles from anywhere. I was much later than I expected to be, and I couldn't telephone your mother. I'm afraid she was worried. How do you like our new car?"

Jim didn't even answer. "Gee, Dad, I'm glad you're all right," he said.

"What's biting you, Jim?" asked his father. "I was about to bawl you out for not putting the spade away. I found it out by the garden."

"Your tree hasn't broken, Mom, has it?" asked Jim anxiously. "As soon as I cool Warrior off I'll prop up that limb for you."

"No, it's not broken," said his mother, looking at him the way she did when she suspected he was coming down with a cold. "What *is* the matter with you?" she asked.

"Nothing," said Jim. "I just found out something, that's all. I've got to walk Warrior. He's hot." And he ran his hand over the horse's sweaty neck.

Riding up to the kennel, he stopped to have a word with the beagles. "I'll take you for a good long ride tomorrow," he promised them. The horse put down his head and the hounds sniffed through the wire as if curious to know where he'd been.

Jim looked down at the four beagles. "I'm glad you're not too fat to run after rabbits," he said. "Poor Weaky! If you could see him now, Lucy, you'd be sorry, you really would.

"Come on, Warrior, we can't stand here any longer or you'll catch cold." Jim gathered up his reins and turned the horse away from the kennel. Riding proud and straight and sitting easily in the saddle, he dropped one hand to Warrior's withers and with his fingers caressed the damp coat. "You're smart," he said, "and I've been so dumb. All the time I was wanting to be someone else, you weren't minding that you had patches or that your sire wasn't a thoroughbred. You just went ahead and did the best you could do. Maybe we can both try doing that now—together!"